THE CREW

JOSEPH KESSEL

THE CREW

Translated by
André Naffis-Sahely

PUSHKIN PRESS
LONDON

Pushkin Press
71–75 Shelton Street
London WC2H 9JQ

First published in French as *L'Équipage*, 1923

First published by Pushkin Press in 2016

This book is supported by the Institut français
(Royaume-Uni) as part of the Burgess programme

1 3 5 7 9 8 6 4 2

ISBN 978 1 782271 61 1

Set in Monotype Baskerville by Tetragon, London

Proudly printed and bound in Great Britain by TJ International,
Padstow, Cornwall on Munken Premium White 80gsm

www.pushkinpress.com

for Sandi

PART ONE

CHAPTER I

THE NEW TRUNK, with its securely fastened leather straps and bearing the freshly painted name *Officer Cadet Jean Herbillon*, was cluttering up the entrance hall.

The father, who was fiddling with the chain of his pocket watch, looked at the time and, rather a little too sternly, said: "We should get going, Jean."

"Are you sure you want to go on your own?" his mother asked. "Like a big boy?"

The young man lowered his gaze to avoid having to see his mother try to force a smile. "Yes, mother," he said. "I'll be brave, and so will you. Besides, don't forget Georges is coming with me."

They stopped talking. The clamour of the street made the silence they were powerless to break seem far more noticeable. They were keen for this goodbye ceremony to be over, for the door to close on this separation, which was tearing them apart on the inside. So intolerable was this moment to them that it made them feel helpless, meaning they could neither admit how anxious they were, nor pretend nothing was wrong.

Jean was counting the seconds, those last, oppressive seconds filled with false sentiments, like his father's stoicism, his mother's bravery, and even his own cheerfulness. The only real, palpable emotion was his parents' all-consuming suffering, and Jean's own impatience to get away from them so he wouldn't have to endure it any longer. He knew that the moment he crossed the threshold, all that sadness would fall from him like a troublesome veil as he joined the race towards the future and a life of action…

A child's voice rang out, striking a triumphal, dissonant note: "The car's here, Jean; I had a hard time finding it, you know."

"I knew I could count on you," the young man told his little brother with a smile.

Jean hurried to leave. Confronted with his family's tense faces, a lump had developed in his throat and he wanted to get away before they could see the colour drain from his face.

A few awkward kisses were exchanged, along with some vain, feverish words.

The brothers drove through streets emptied by the night and the wartime curfew. A bluish glow leaked out of the streetlights, which had been fitted with slotted covers. Inside the dimly lit car, the little one turned to look at Jean and couldn't decide what he most admired in him: his courage, the winged stars on his collar or the shininess of the tawny leather. As far as Georges was concerned, Jean was the living embodiment of war, such as he'd seen it illustrated in all the pictures and posters.

The young man slowly savoured that adulation, especially since his own self-image was just as naive.

He was twenty years old. It was his first tour of duty on the front. Despite all the stories he'd heard at boot camp and his own keen sense of reality, his youth couldn't think of war without endowing it with all the trappings of heroism.

Once they reached the Gare de l'Est, Jean straightened his kepi, put his peacoat on and said to Georges: "Take the trunk to the train bound for Jonchery and wait for me."

The platforms were teeming with soldiers. The joy of their leave from the front was still imprinted on their faces. Jean walked past groups of these soldiers, his heart swelling with comradely pride. He could finally consider himself the equal of those who were about to depart. He loved them for all they had suffered, especially those whom death had already marked out. Since he believed that he too carried that precious essence within him that evening, he felt he could also bask in a little of that love and respect.

From time to time, his thoughts strayed to that city drowning in darkness, which filled him with a disdainful pity. That city only sheltered men who were either unable or unwilling to fight. He, on the other hand, now walked among the warriors.

He felt a pair of arms wrap themselves around him. Then his senses were engulfed by a familiar perfume.

"Jean, my darling," a breathless, trembling voice muttered. "I was so worried I wouldn't make it in time."

Jean turned his eyes, which were still intoxicated with that naive image of himself, towards the young woman and said: "I knew you'd come."

His tone was calm, almost indifferent, but it concealed a deep tenderness, and an even deeper pride. Without Denise there, his departure simply wouldn't have been as glorious.

How invigorating she was! It was the only word he could find to describe his mistress. Her skin, her eyes, her voice, her laughter, her feelings, they were all invigorating!

The young woman slid her arm into his and, pressing tightly against him, they walked, cutting through the crowds of washed-out greatcoats.

With Denise beside him, Jean wasn't counting the seconds like he'd done at home. He felt more carefree while next to her. Despite his imminent departure, despite the front he already belonged to, and whose tentacles seemed to move inside those darkened trains, he felt as though their rendezvous could last forever. The ease of their union seemed to banish all other anxieties.

A whistle pierced through the cacophony of the station. Denise pressed herself tighter against the young man and this told him they were about to part ways. He detected neither fear nor sorrow in his mistress's eyes, just a muted adoration. He bent down to meet her mouth and, although he knew it was a farewell kiss, and that it could also be their last, given that they might never see one another again, his young body buckled under those firm lips.

They ran towards the rumbling train. Men who'd been torn from the city's peaceful embrace were leaning against the doors. Georges was anxiously searching through the multitude of sullied uniforms to spot his brother's silhouette: dazzling like a piece of polished metal. When he finally saw him, in the company of a young woman, Georges shouted in perhaps too militaristic a tone: "Your trunk's been loaded, Jean. Quick, get on."

The train cars were shuddering. Jean roughly shook his brother's hand, kissed his mistress's fingers, and jumped on the footboard just as the train was departing. He tried to be as graceful as possible in that single motion since he so dearly desired to keep playing a certain role.

Jean was surprised to find his compartment was full of civilians. It seemed so odd and appalling to him that men would travel for work or pleasure on the same train that was leading him to danger. He'd assumed he would be travelling with officers, comrades who belonged to the heroic school which he believed the front to be. Instead, he found himself in the presence of a small, wrinkled old man, three preppy teenage boys and a young woman whose bearing was a little too formal in contrast to her affectionate eyes.

Nevertheless, his disappointment led him to realize the new perks he could now enjoy. Sat in the corner seat his brother had reserved for him, Jean unceremoniously crossed his leather-clad legs and began smoking a pipe, which always kept going out because he'd never learned how to use an accessory which he'd deemed essential to his new persona.

The train, that fiery river, sped alongside shadowy banks. Jean's gaze occasionally met the young woman's, who would look away after a brief smile. Her teeth were a pearly white. The rim of her hat cast a mysterious penumbra that covered her face almost all the way down to her lips, but he could see that her breasts were firm and loose underneath her silk blouse. This image alone awakened a desire for sexual conquest in Jean, and his face beamed with such unrestrained lust that the old man shot him a complicit smile. Yet, lowering her eyelids, the unknown woman pretended to go to sleep. Disappointed, Jean stepped out into the corridor.

He leaned his forehead against the window's metal bar. Lights flickered across the plain. Streams and rivers shone like pieces of luminous silk. In the midst of the train's excitement, Jean could almost hear the impetuous uproar of his desire: to get there, to join his squadron. Over the course of the past year, Jean's youthful pride and his thirst for glory and danger had turned those goals into his sole purpose in life. Now that he was a cadet-observer, and had flown a dozen flights at the Le Plessis airbase, knew all the marshalling signals and had learned Morse code, he was itching to take his place among the supermen he'd pictured, certain he would be able to prove his worthiness.

He was so lost in his daydreaming that he didn't hear his compartment gradually emptying out and he gave a little start when a voice very close to him asked: "Will we reach Fismes soon, Monsieur?"

He noticed the woman whom he'd given up on seducing was standing next to him, almost touching his shoulder. All his dreams and memories suddenly vanished. As the question had been asked in a non-committal tone that didn't require an exact answer, Jean answered hers with one of his own: "You know you're travelling very close to the front lines, Madame?"

"My uncle is waiting for me."

Her smile made it all too obvious that she didn't care whether he believed in the existence of this uncle.

They went back inside their compartment. Jean offered her a cigarette and she accepted. She laughed easily and her vocabulary was fairly common, albeit lively. Jean quickly realized she was on her way to join an army commander whom she didn't really like, but who supported her financially. After a few demurs on her part, he won the privilege of addressing her by her first name, which was Nelly, and Jean wanted to press his advantage.

But the memory of his mistress put a stop to his plans. She had been so sweet and loyal. Was he going to betray her now, having just barely left her? Yet a decisive line of argument banished all his scruples. Tomorrow he would be at the front. Thus, didn't he have a right to fulfil all his desires? He took the young woman in his arms. She didn't resist.

When Nelly left, a gentle weariness overcame the young officer cadet as he savoured the memory of an easy triumph. Suddenly, he felt as though a shadow had sat next to him. He shuddered and looked around. There was nobody there. Neither was there anyone out in the corridor, or in the rest of the car for that matter. Only a great silence, broken by a few bumps and jolts. Jean realized his loneliness had assumed a bodily form.

The train rolled along fearfully and cautiously, the night-lights had been lit, and the darkness outside was as dense as black marble. As though he'd only just understood the full meaning of the word, the young man exclaimed: "The front!"

Pressing his face against the windowpane, he vainly tried to glimpse through the darkness, whose immense cloak concealed all the nearby trenches and the hundreds of thousands of men who lived in a state of alert.

He felt as though a thump resounded in his chest.

"Artillery fire," he murmured, as though having experienced another revelation.

Tense, Jean kept his ears pricked, as though unwilling to miss even the slightest noise of breath coming out of those unknown lands. He'd left Paris only a few hours earlier. He thought he could still see his parents' faces, or feel the flesh of his mistress's arm, and could still remember the colourful display of the news kiosk at the station. Yet at the same time he already felt bound to this new place, where men died in droves. Through the same window which had once framed Denise's face, Jean could now see the gloomy, secret outline of the front.

The train proceeded slowly, almost gently, as though aware of how enfeebled its passengers had become. The train's rocking motion and silence—albeit a silence punctuated by a distant rumble—meant the ecstasy that had made the young man giddy ever since his departure finally disappeared. Soon enough, all he could feel was an anxious solitude and strange questions insinuated their way into his doubtful mind. Why did he have to enlist? Why did he have to pick the most dangerous branch in the army?

He recalled the image of the burning aircraft which had crashed close to the aviation school's grounds and thought about how his own flesh might one day crackle and sizzle like that.

Why was that odious train rolling along so slowly? It was like it was loaded with coffins! And that bland, colourless lantern light, and that field completely subsumed by the night!

Jean now began to criticize himself. He was fully aware of what had pushed him towards enlisting in the air force. It hadn't been his thirst for heroism, but his vanity. He'd allowed himself to be seduced by the glamour of the uniforms, those flashy winged stars and the prestige pilots enjoyed among women. Women had been the decisive factor. His breast swelled with hatred for those feeble, perverse creatures for whom he'd given up his life. Since she hadn't attempted to dissuade him, Denise seemed the most despicable of them all.

Looking for other grievances to bear a grudge over, he realized he didn't really know much about that young woman: didn't know who her friends were, hadn't visited her home, and didn't even know her surname. He also realized he didn't have a single portrait of her, and that he'd only discovered she was married because she'd once forgotten to remove her wedding band. This mystery, which had until that point made Denise seem so compelling, had then turned into a mark of dishonesty and coldness.

Jean thought about how his brief adventure with Nelly had been a means to achieve his just revenge and tried to allay his anxieties by revelling in that memory.

The train, meanwhile, had slowed to the point that one might well have walked beside it. Jean wanted to get off so he could lose that unbearable weight which was oppressing him, and this very desire revealed the full extent of his distress.

"I'm scared," he thought, in spite of himself.

He tried to defend himself, but all the arguments withered away in the face of his self-loathing. What would be the point of lying to himself? All his indignation against himself or Denise had been caused by that very fear.

The young man who'd laughed when he'd talked about danger, who'd called those who seemed to understand the word "fear" a bunch of cowards, he, Officer

Cadet Jean Herbillon, was now scared himself, and this had happened even before he'd come anywhere close to danger.

Jean experienced such shame that he didn't even realize it completely neutralized his fear.

CHAPTER II

THE SUN'S BROADSWORD pierced through Jean's eyelids. He turned on his side, jealously guarding his sleep, but then the roof started to shake and it made him rise to his feet still dazed by the light and noise.

His eyes first fell on the empty room and the shelf where a pitcher of water lay, although he didn't understand what he was looking at. What was that sombre cage upholstered in tar paper? However, the sight of his trunk, still unpacked, proved to be the missing link that reforged his chain of memories. He had joined his squadron.

He jumped out of bed and threw his uniform on. The noise that had woken him up had come from an engine. They were already flying; he must have woken up late. Despairing, he thought the others would think he was lazy. At that exact moment, a soldier as huge and clumsy as a bear painfully squeezed his frame through the narrow door.

"I'm the orderly," he said. "Would my lieutenant like some hot water? Then I'll bring the coffee."

The soldier was blind in one eye, which made the young officer awkward. Hesitantly, he said: "No, thank you. I would prefer some cold water."

Then he reflected and forced himself to add: "You should have woken me up earlier."

"The captain said I should let my lieutenant sleep," the soldier replied, winking at Jean with his one good eye.

"Ah, the captain…" Jean murmured.

"He's a man who knows what's what," the orderly calmly continued. "The lieutenant will have all the time he needs for everything."

The officer cadet liked the orderly's friendly, familiar tone, but thought it best that the soldier also respect him.

"That's good," he curtly replied. "I won't be having any breakfast this morning."

The sun and that deafening noise which kept stopping and then furiously starting again, which he now recognized as the sound of whirling propellers, were luring him to the outside world. When he stepped outside his room, he left the darkness behind. He found himself in a long, narrow, shadowy corridor with two rows of doors on either side. Noticing light filtering through one of the doors to his left, he walked towards it.

He entered a large room which, thanks to its four windows, was filled with the clear light of day. It was upholstered in corrugated cardboard and, standing in front of a long table, which was covered with a white wax-cloth studded with blue flowers, Jean felt both cheerful and invigorated. He was examining a stack of shelves that filled one of the corners of the room when he heard: "So you've already discovered the bar, Mr Officer Cadet. Your future looks promising already."

The voice was so refined, sharp-edged and full of cheer that it reverberated through Jean's body like a benign wave. He spun around. Standing in front of the corridor's dark gaping mouth was a young man with his arms held behind his back. He was dressed in a black tunic whose cloth shone just as much as its gold buttons. The tunic closely hugged his thin waist and narrow neck. The fine slenderness of his frame matched the sharp features of his face: his bright, almond-shaped eyes, his straight nose and the pencil moustache that was framed by the corners of his lips.

"He isn't much older than me," the young officer cadet told himself, "and he doesn't have any medals on his chest: he must be new here too."

Glad to have met a comrade who didn't intimidate him, giving him some time before coming face to face with his senior officers, Jean casually introduced himself: "Officer Cadet Jean Herbillon."

"Captain Gabriel Thélis, squadron commander," the young man replied.

The captain held out his hand and Jean noticed three tarnished gold service stripes on his sleeve. Jean felt his cheeks were ripe to burst thanks to a sudden rush of blood to the head, and the feeling that his skin was on fire only served to increase his terrible confusion.

Forgetting that he wasn't wearing his kepi, Jean raised his hand to his forehead and stammered: "Forgive me, Captain."

A flurry of agonizing thoughts flashed through his mind. He'd behaved like a goofy popinjay. Instead of expressing the admiration he now felt for this young captain, he'd addressed him with insupportable familiarity. He thought he'd lost all credibility in the captain's eyes.

While Jean stood stiffly with his brow all sweaty, the captain's eyes—now endowed with a golden sheen by the sunlight—never shifted from the officer cadet. Suddenly, the room filled with clear, hearty laughter.

Firm fingers came to rest on Herbillon's shoulder and the voice that boomed with well-being told him: "Enough formalities. Let's go see the planes."

Soon enough they were walking the grounds just outside the barracks. Surrounded by the clear contours of a road, and fringed by a curtain of trees in the distance, the field ahead was large and flat, before it came to a stop in front of two abrupt cliffs that spoiled the entire landscape. From a chasm hollowed out by the river to the north rose a bluish vapour, while to the south lay the greyish smoke of human dwellings. Jean was thus able to get his bearings and plot where the river Vesle ran through and where the village of Rosny-sous-Bois lay. He didn't linger on this. His gaze hungrily wanted to absorb everything that this landscape, indicative of a risky life, contained. He went to see immense hangars that looked like truncated cathedrals, groups of mechanics scattered here and there, the huge white canvas T-shaped weathervane which indicated the wind's direction. Much to his surprise, he found that this war-zone closely resembled the aviation school where he'd undergone his training.

Nevertheless, Captain Thélis was still examining him. The captain had liked Jean from the get-go, despite his outrageously new peacoat and his useless leather harness. He liked the frankness of his face, his forehead, which seemed indicative of willpower, his eyes, which beamed with candour, and the vitality that animated his entire body. Yet Captain Thélis could only express his sympathy for the officer cadet through jokes. "So you're not a morning person, eh rookie?" he said, all of a sudden.

Jean jumped with a start.

"I know," the captain continued, "you got here late. Still, if I'd been in your shoes I would have woken up at dawn to see your comrades off."

Jean didn't dare tell him what the orderly had said and instead hung his head. Ruthlessly continuing his jesting, the captain carried on: "A little dumb, are we? Fine, tell me what they taught you at school."

"But… well, everything, Captain."

"That's too much."

Offended, Herbillon expounded what he'd been taught: how to use the wireless, calibrating the flight controls, photography…

The captain interrupted him. "Do you know how to *look*?" he said.

This time, the officer cadet thought the captain was joking, but Thélis's curtness wiped the smile off his face.

"I don't mean to be funny," he said. "Let me assure you, here we learn how to really look. It just takes time."

He carried on questioning Jean over several technical details, and to each of Jean's answers the captain muttered: "We'll see, we'll see, it's not as easy as that."

Yet the captain never posed the question Jean most wanted to answer—whether he was brave or not. In fact, Thélis didn't even hint at it. Herbillon was hurt by this: he saw it as an unceremonious slight. The fear he'd felt the previous day had completely dissipated and, standing on that sunny plateau where the fresh air filled men with the desire to fly, Officer Cadet Jean Herbillon believed himself immune to fear. Thus, he wanted to prove himself.

"When can I fly, Captain?" he asked, looking like the cat that got the cream.

"If the weather's good tomorrow I'll take you up myself," Thélis answered, seemingly completely unfazed by the question.

"Over the front lines?" Jean insisted.

"No, over Monte Carlo."

Despite the captain's mockery, Herbillon added: "We'll fight, won't we, Captain?"

Thélis looked at him with a sort of mocking tenderness. "I really hope we won't," he said. "If we engaged the enemy on each sortie then we'd be out of business!"

The young man repressed his surprise and disappointment, but the captain had guessed exactly what the officer cadet was feeling: his desire to display his bravery, to fulfil his ambitions of glory and battle, his faith in daily feats of prowess. The captain recalled his own arrival at the squadron three years earlier, and how the exact same thoughts he'd detected in Herbillon's eyes had once flashed through his own mind. He wanted to explain it all to him, but he knew the young officer cadet wouldn't believe him, so he said to himself: "He's a good recruit."

He didn't realize he was actually praising the young lieutenant he'd once been and not the cadet standing in front of him.

"You've got guts, I'm sure of that," the captain kindly told him. "The rookies are always braver than the rest of us, who've all become jaded!"

The captain suddenly frowned, cast a quick glance on the field and quickly headed towards a group of men who had assembled in front of a hangar. So as not to be left alone in the middle of a field where he didn't know anyone, Herbillon followed him.

They soon found themselves outside the Bessonneau hangar, a white canvas structure with a bell-shaped roof, where through its high nave one could glimpse the confused mass of aeroplanes. Some mechanics were standing around nonchalantly, absorbed in chatter. A bulky lieutenant was sitting in their midst, smoking a very old pipe atop an oil drum. When the captain arrived, the men stood to attention; not budging an inch, the officer smiled broadly. He said: "Fine weather we've having, eh old chap? Not flying today?"

He stretched, perfectly blissful.

"So, you're on your sunbathing shift?" The captain suddenly yelled: "Look up there!"

There was anger in his voice and in his sombre gaze, and Jean was surprised to watch the affable, mocking young man transform into a stern officer. However, the bulky lieutenant didn't make the slightest move. Following the spot Thélis had indicated, he lifted his eyes to glance at the wind tee on top of a hangar and calmly replied:

"That damned breeze changes all the time."

He beckoned to two men and headed over to the gigantic T in order to change its direction. On his return, Thélis grumbled: "Fat lizard."

Then he turned to Jean and said: "Herbillon, meet Marbot, my old comrade and the chief observer here, and the very best there is."

The officer cadet immediately respected the lieutenant given the captain had recommended him so highly, and worried that the lieutenant would resent being reprimanded in front of a rookie. But the bulky man said: "Thanks for being here, young fellow. I suspect Thélis didn't want to ruin my reputation in front of you, otherwise he would have been far crueler."

Thélis couldn't help himself and burst out laughing.

"You know me well, you old dog," he muttered; then he asked. "Has Berthier been gone a long time?"

"Roughly a couple of hours, Captain," one of the mechanics answered.

"He should have been back by now, I assigned him a quick reconnaissance mission."

Marbot, who'd resumed his place on the oil drum, grimaced in disgust.

"Some people can't get enough of it."

"That's true," Thélis concurred distractedly.

He looked up at the sky, which was a pale blue. The horizon trembled in the wan light. Marbot shrugged.

"You want to fly too, huh? There are no missions today."

"I'm going to try out my new engine."

Herbillon cast a supplicating gaze at the captain. "Take me with you, Captain," he asked.

"I told you: tomorrow," Thélis drily answered. "I thought I made myself clear. In the meanwhile, study the maps; you can make yourself useful that way."

As the captain headed towards his plane, Marbot told Jean:

"Don't worry old chap, Thélis is the very best we've got but he's afraid he's too young for people to obey him. That's all."

Herbillon had never imagined that an aviator could be as bulky and scruffy as Marbot. He was wearing a filthy blue uniform that was far too large for him, and which hung loosely off his sturdy limbs; a grey army sweater enveloped his torso and neck and his feet ambled sweetly along in a pair of clogs. With his chipped pipe stuck firmly between his little yellow teeth, he looked like a peaceful farmer shooting the breeze after a hard day's work.

As though he'd guessed what the young man was thinking, Marbot said: "Being comfortable is your chief priority. All you need is a bedroom, an experienced cook, a pipe, and you're set. I'll teach you all of that. You just need to be a little organized and you'll get by just fine on your army pay."

He began to explain how he thought Herbillon should budget. At the mess hall, officer cadets only spent three francs a day. Marbot would give him a pair of trousers and an army jacket, which a tailor could resize, so that he wouldn't have to use his new uniform. After he'd bought some tobacco, he would still have enough left over to put some money aside.

Jean listened to Marbot, afraid that he was also making fun of him. To think that these were the first recommendations his commanding officer had given him! They were standing on a field burning with feverish heroism and here he was talking about household finances. He was trying to provoke him!

But no, the bulky lieutenant wasn't kidding. Marbot's cheeks swelled with a kind of affection while he calculated the sums the young officer cadet could spend while on leave from the front. Then he stopped talking, as though he had nothing else to say to the young man. Despite his run of bad luck with the captain, Jean ventured, "And as for work, what would you advise me to do?"

Marbot savoured a big puff of his pipe and answered: "Nothing. You'll pick it up as you go along."

A wild whirring noise twisted his features into a grimace. "That's Thélis making all that noise," he grumbled. "Go have a look, old chap—it must still be a fun sight for you."

The captain's happy head emerged out of the cockpit. The force of the propellers was ruffling his short black hair, and curled his lips into a silent laugh. Sometimes he slowed the engine down; at others he gave it full throttle. The aeroplane twitched like an impatient beast, just like its pilot, both lusting after the vastness of space.

Thélis finally jumped off and hit the ground. As he'd put on a pair of blue overalls to try out the engine, he looked like one of the mechanics surrounding the plane, with whom he started to swap jokes. Then he walked towards Jean and asked: "What time is it?"

"Just after twelve, Captain."

"And Berthier still isn't here; that beast is going to start worrying me."

The word made Jean feel strangely pleased. It was the first time he'd been reminded he was actually stationed at the front, and it justified his pride and dreams. Danger had finally shown its true face. He was almost disappointed when Marbot, having scanned the sky with his small, piercing eyes, had spotted an object that had looked invisible to Jean and called out:

"There he is, Captain."

A biplane swerved to the right above the field and its landing gear grazed the ground. The pilot was the first to climb down. He was wearing his flight suit and leather helmet, with his goggles resting on his forehead. He looked like a deep-sea diver of the skies. Jean couldn't make out any of his features except for a scar that ran all the way from his mouth to the edge of his aviator hood. He was limping.

"Taking your time, eh Deschamps!" the captain yelled.

The pilot replied in a drawl typical of people from the Touraine countryside. "Berthier wanted to look at everything."

He removed his helmet. His mouth was disfigured by the wine-red scar running to his ear. He was badly shaven and his blond fuzz gave his huge face an ochre sheen. Jean found him unpleasant, but when the pilot removed his suit, Jean was stunned to see his chest studded with glorious medals and ribbons.

He was distracted by a strange silhouette. A body rose out of the observer's seat on the biplane and, even though he was wrapped in wools and furs, he still looked very thin. Each of his movements was accompanied by a clicking sound. In his hands was what looked like an excessive stack of wooden and nickel plates. A great number of instruments whose uses Jean knew nothing of were hanging from his shoulder and the various pockets located around his suit. Even his cork helmet and goggles had an unusual shape to them.

Jean noticed that everyone around him, from the captain all the way to the mechanics, smiled at this man with a mixture of irony and tenderness, which increased when Thélis called out to him and asked: "So, Berthier, have you finally cracked the laws of perpetual motion by spending all that time up there?"

A voice suddenly arose from the observer's hood that instantly inspired a tender sweetness in Jean, even though he couldn't understand why. It rang out with a naive, stirring clarity, embodying a captivating innocence that made such childish ways of talking seem so charming. It said: "Forgive me, Captain, I completely lost track of time. There was a blank spot in the Trench of Cannibals that I wanted to identify at all costs."

"And?"

"I couldn't manage it; I'll get it done next time."

Marbot shook his head gravely.

"Pierre, Pierre, you dishonour me…"

"Is that so, big guy?" Berthier exclaimed. "Would you believe it!…"

"Oh no," Thélis exclaimed. "If you get started we'll be here until nightfall, and we're hungry! Get yourself over to the office, file your report and be prepared to pay the late fines."

Deschamps, who was carefully inspecting his camera, swiped a misshapen thumb across his brow and noted:

"This sortie is going to cost us dearly, four tears on our wings."

"Four? Were you in a fight?"

Jean was startled.

"No, it must have been artillery fire," Deschamps said.

"Well, there we have it, you're up to speed now, Herbillon," the captain cried. "We'll drink a bottle for each bullet hole."

"Ah, this heathen here won't want to hear any jokes like that," Marbot grumbled, "but that's where all his money is going to go!"

*

The evening of that first day with his squadron, Herbillon returned to his room, drunk with exhaustion.

The conversations at the table were still ringing in his ears like a volley of bullets; ten faces, which he hadn't known up until that day, had been etched into his mind with haunting precision. He tried to put a name to each of them but couldn't manage it. The names of those he'd met on the field—the captain, Marbot, scar-face Deschamps, Berthier's childish voice with his head always in the clouds—instead came easily to him.

He also remembered Doc, the pilot-physician who wore his golden wings on his facing, which was made from garnet-red velvet. One face in particular had left an impression: a great beak of a nose, a drooping moustache, he looked like an old D'Artagnan—then there was another: a clean-shaven face, haughty, and pale.

Yet they all shared a common characteristic: a slightly crazed look in their eyes, a feverish light that illuminated all their faces, which manifested itself regardless of whether they were calm or nervous, fierce or depressed, a kind of prayer that rose from those devil-may-care men.

Thélis's eyes burned with passion, while Berthier's gaze was dreamy; Deschamps's was lacklustre, while Marbot's was jolly; yet all were inhabited by that vague flame, which befuddled them and stirred them up, one after the other. Jean examined his face in the mirror and a great sense of pride warmed his veins: he thought he could recognize the same strange comradely look in his own eyes.

He felt suddenly reassured. That look in his eyes contradicted the remarks that had so disconcerted him the previous day. His comrades had only talked about their pay, wine, leave from the front and women. Their eyes betrayed an adventurous twinkle. They were certainly jaded, but only because they'd achieved so many exploits. Whereas he'd just joined the saga. Tomorrow, the captain would take him flying, and there would doubtlessly be a fight; they might even shoot down an enemy plane.

He had already started drafting the letter he would send to Denise.

The army cot, narrow and stiff, felt delightfully restful to his limbs, which had been strained by standing in the field all day and in the mess hall all evening. Everything that came easily and naturally to the others instead required all the effort at his body's disposal. He kept paying attention to his slightest move, how he walked, how he talked; he was even afraid of coming across as too shy or unpleasant. All that effort had left him irritated rather than tired and, despite his exhaustion, he only fell asleep very late.

Opening his eyes to the milky light, he thought morning still hadn't broken. All the thoughts that had subconsciously invaded his sleep, returned to him in a flash, like a confused, joyful halo: today he was going to fly. Mathieu the orderly entered his room with a pitcher of steaming water.

"How?" Jean exclaimed, looking around for his watch.

"It's ten in the morning," the soldier said. "Given the state of the weather, I didn't wake you up. The ground's like molasses out there, Lieutenant."

"But it was so nice yesterday," Jean muttered.

"The weather turns quickly over here, sir, we might still get a little sunshine later on. In fact, Lieutenant, soon enough you might welcome a bit of fog in the morning, just like everyone else here."

On that note, the orderly left, leaving Herbillon to his despair. He'd so dearly hoped to fly that morning and thus be initiated into the squadron! At which point he could have stood shoulder to shoulder with the "veterans" around him, or at least felt he was their younger comrade.

Whereas he would be forced to remain a novice for the time being, nothing but a rookie.

His eyes examined the room, which he hadn't had the time to do the previous day. He shuddered at the sight: a black open coffin framed by a window curtained with a pale misty cloth.

"I can't live like this," he thought to himself. "I've got to brighten up the walls somehow."

This sudden desire allowed him to shake off his idleness and he got out of bed, feeling a little less crestfallen.

As he entered again with a cup of coffee, Mathieu asked: "Would the lieutenant like a pair of clogs?"

"Oh, no!" Jean exclaimed disdainfully, remembering Marbot's dishevelled appearance.

Yet at the same time Jean couldn't see the point of lacing up his boots, given that the state of his room and the filthy-looking morning outside, didn't exactly make him aspire to any elegance.

"Does everyone wear them?" he asked, somewhat hesitantly.

"Nearly, Lieutenant."

"Bring me a pair," Jean ordered him.

He was rummaging around in his trunk to find some photographs and engravings so he could brighten up those unbearable tarred walls when someone gently knocked on his door. As he thought it was the orderly, he didn't turn around. Yet a voice, which he instantly recognized due to its charming timbre, asked him: "Am I bothering you, Monsieur?"

By way of reply, Jean gave Berthier a hearty handshake. The lieutenant was wrapped in a goatskin which he'd thrown on top of his grey cloth pyjamas.

"You must be bored. The first few days here are always difficult."

"That's right, I am."

The answer had risen to his lips without Jean being able to restrain it, and yet he saw it as an admission of weakness he wouldn't have confessed to anyone else. Nevertheless, even though he didn't know Berthier, Jean realized he couldn't keep his real emotions from him, provided, of course, they were genuine. He'd felt this as soon as he'd seen him climb down from his cockpit.

"I see you've dressed already," Berthier continued. "You'll get the hang of it soon enough. You'll pick up our lazy habits eventually. They help us live more comfortably."

Jean followed him down the corridor, which was swarming with busy orderlies, and entered a room that was for all accounts and purposes identical to his own except for an oil stove that puffed out a warm, acrid breath. Various items of clothing hung dishevelled on the walls, while there were astonishing piles of little bits of wood and metal—barbed wire, scraps of cloth, screws, nuts and bolts, punctured tyres—scattered everywhere: on top of the large rough-topped table, on top of the poorly nailed shelves, on top of the stools and even on top of the bed.

Having displayed the chaos of his room, Berthier smiled like a man apologizing for what he knew was an obsession, yet one he was nonetheless very fond of.

"This is my warehouse," he explained. "I bring everything I find on the field here that I can use to build, to invent."

Then, despite himself, he grew livelier: "Needless to say, people make fun of me. But look at this, it's a special cartridge extractor for machine guns that the entire squadron now uses. And people say this set of expandable and collapsible boards that can be used for cards is impractical, but once I perfect it everyone is going to want one. Obviously, this means my room's become a little cramped thanks to everything I store here, but I can assure you that it's most practical."

He started to laugh and then added: "Thélis mocks me the most."

"But you like him, don't you?" Jean asked, noticing the warmth with which he'd pronounced the captain's name.

"Of course, I love him dearly," his comrade replied. "You see, my friend, everyone here would gladly die for him. I don't know how to explain it. That twenty-four-year-old boy is the life and soul of this squadron. His joy, his courage, his youth! He was awarded a flying cross as an observer, and six medals as a pilot, but he never even mentions it! He would fly ten-hour missions every day if we let him. And what a good comrade he is, you'll see!"

Berthier's paean swelled, surrounding the officer's face, which had moved the young man at first sight, with a glorious aura.

"What about the others?" Jean asked.

"All very charming, but Thélis is on a different level. And we all know it."

They talked for a long time. Jean gradually began to be acquainted with his comrades: there was Deschamps the country bumpkin, an infantry soldier who received an honourable discharge after being wounded, then joined the air force, then was discharged a second time after his biplane rolled over in the evening mist, shattering his ribs, ripping off a thumb, and disfiguring his face, at which point he re-enlisted for a third time and shot down three enemy planes. Then there was Captain Reuillard, an observer who'd joined up after seeing service in the army wagon-trains and was an old choleric soldier. André de Neuville, who was very cold, very unforgiving, arrogant and valiant, was the least loved of the bunch. Fat Marbot was a career officer, an old infantry sergeant major who'd joined the air force simply because the enlistment premium would allow him to marry a Normandy farm girl. Marbot was a peaceful man who didn't like exposing himself to unnecessary risks and who, when the occasion called for it, was the most reliable and courageous of all the observers.

Berthier talked about them all with unforced benevolence, and with each passing moment, Jean became fonder and fonder of him.

The lunch bell interrupted their conversation.

"I have to get dressed right away," Berthier exclaimed. "The captain doesn't like it when we're late."

Entering the mess hall where several officers had already assembled, Jean Herbillon was greeted by a unanimous cry. "Officer Cadet—to the bar!"

Having no idea as to what was going on, he was informed that the youngest among them was tasked with the duty of filling their glasses and keeping tracks of all the bar tabs.

Shaken up, stunned, yet cheered by that growing familiarity, he took his place behind the bar shelves that were stacked with bottles.

The officers' mouths drank their booze neat and talked loudly. The newspapers had just arrived and the news from Paris fuelled the discussions, but everything was bathed in that cheerful, carefree hubbub that is the prerogative of students and soldiers. The clamour was still growing unabated when the captain appeared.

"About time!" he said when he noticed Jean standing at the bar. "We respect our traditions here. One vermouth rookie, and don't skimp on the booze when it comes to the senior officers."

At that moment, Marbot's frame darkened the threshold of the corridor's entrance. He was wearing a sweater. Thélis rushed towards him and yelled: "No grease monkeys in here."

With his ink-coloured pipe between his teeth, Marbot sighed: "But I'm so comfortable without my jacket."

"Pay the fine then!" Deschamps exclaimed.

"No!" the bulky lieutenant said, looking truly distressed. "You can't do that to me!"

"Then get dressed, you filthy beast!" Thélis pitilessly ordered him.

Once Marbot returned, Deschamps proposed: "By the way, Captain, we should show the rookie our squadron's quadrille."

Herbillon was suddenly grabbed by some strong arms, hoisted up over the bar and then swept along by the bawdy rhythms of a wild round dance, which didn't come to a halt until the first dishes arrived.

Once sitting at the table, Jean continued to learn about his duties as an officer cadet. One of them was to read out the menu, but Thélis warned him, in all seriousness, that he would have to make it rhyme the next time he did so. Jean was the butt of all jokes and was constantly threatened with endless chores. That barrage of ridicule made him feel proud and happy, because it constituted his first real link to that tightly knit group of men, which he badly wanted to belong to.

By the end of the meal, Jean had become so accustomed to his new role that when the phone rang he immediately rushed to it. The army corps wanted to speak to the squadron commander.

Thélis commanded the room's silence with a single gesture and picked up the receiver.

The captain's increasingly worried features replaced the previously cheerful expressions on everyone's face with restless concern. Thélis suddenly exclaimed: "But considering the fog that would be impossible at this time, Colonel."

A new silence settled over the room. Everyone knew that thanks to the invisible phone line's witchcraft, decisions that would determine their fate had been made somewhere far away. Thélis continued: "I can assure you it's sheer madness, Colonel."

Then: "We'll try, Colonel, but I can't give you any certainties and I'll only ask my men to volunteer for the mission. Otherwise I'll need an official order."

He loudly slammed the receiver back on the hook and Jean started to hear whispers whose meaning he couldn't grasp. "Naturally those gentlemen don't have a doubt in their minds."

"It's always the same with headquarters."

"They should try having a steering stick between their legs for just a day!"

"If at least they weren't so completely blind!"

Meanwhile, the captain had approached a window

and was looking at the murky sky. He was angrily clenching his teeth, distorting his mouth. He was clearly finding it difficult to speak.

He finally headed over to the table and curtly said: "They think troops are massing on the other side. The general wants us to go and take a look."

"So all he has to do is tell his driver to take him there," Marbot grumbled.

"Shut up!" Thélis harshly yelled at him. "You saw how strongly I objected; there was nothing I could do."

Then, lowering his voice as though he were ashamed, he added: "And Marbot and I have been forbidden to go on this mission, because… because… that's just how it is."

His last words betrayed a great deal of rage, and everyone knew why. Flying in that kind of fog was highly dangerous, and the general didn't want to put his senior officers at risk.

"So I need two of our best men," Thélis continued. "I can't dump this mission on the non-commissioned officers."

There were three pilots in the mess hall: Doc, who'd just arrived, as well as André de Neuville and Deschamps. Jean was certain the latter would rush to answer the captain's call. But the disfigured man kept staring at the table and grumbled as though he were being tortured. "I can't do this, captain," he said. "I'll take on twenty Krauts if I have to, but don't make me go out in that fog."

Herbillon remembered that frightening episode Berthier had told him about when Deschamps's biplane rolled over in the mist.

So Neuville stood up without a word and headed over to the hangar, whose grey, bulky mass seemed like a shapeless outgrowth of the mist. They still needed an observer. Marbot left the room and shouted: "I don't want to watch this. The flight visibility can't be more than thirty metres."

Thélis's eyes saw the humble prayer in Herbillon's gaze, and he tenderly told him: "No kid, you wouldn't do us much good up there."

Jean suffered his inexperience as though it caused him unbearable shame, but by that time, Berthier had already come forward: "Captain, I'm the most senior officer here after Marbot."

"No, not you," Thélis exclaimed. "I…"

What he wanted to say was "I love you too dearly", but his deep commitment to his role as the squadron's commander forced him to restrain his tenderness.

"Go ahead old chap," he told him, firmly.

An engine started to roar outside.

The entire squadron saw them off, even all the unenlisted workers had shown up, and their stunned eyes looked incredulously at the horizon, which was hung so close that it blocked all visibility past the edge of the plateau, after which everything was obfuscated by the fog's denseness.

The mechanics, who were leaning against the wings, thus restraining its momentum, were just about to let go when Thélis leaped up in one bound until he was face to face with Berthier, who was sat in his cockpit, and said: "If the flight visibility is this poor while you're over enemy lines I forbid you to go any further. You hear me?"

Neuville gestured his consent. Freed from all constraints, the biplane lifted off and was almost immediately engulfed by the fog. All the assembled groups scattered, except for Thélis, who was determined to stay on the field until his comrades' return, and Jean, who didn't want to leave the captain on his own.

Neuville hadn't been able to get enough altitude. After he'd barely lifted off the ground, he'd already tasted the bland fog on his lips. Immediately after take-off, such a thick layer of condensation had settled on his windscreen that he'd been forced to lower it. The wind lashing against his forehead sometimes dispersed the fog into little clouds, which he would then chase, as though they were runaway mares. Neuville could see patches of green and brown below, but the fog's milky curtain would soon conceal them from sight again. He pulled his hood down to his nose and lowered his helmet down to his eyebrows, and suddenly thought to himself: "I must be the spitting image of a coward right now under this mask."

He was afraid. Mortally afraid. All his comrades thought he was fearless, but only he alone knew how easily fear infected every part of his body.

Fear was his dark, constant companion. He couldn't even climb into his cockpit without feeling anxious; in fact he couldn't even think about flying without his heart suddenly feeling heavier and slower.

Unable to accept that a man of his breeding and elegance should live in a muddy morass of spilled guts, he had asked to be assigned to the air force as a pilot, the most dangerous job of all, where his pride dictated he take even more risks than he was already exposed to.

His fingers clutching the biplane's controls, he headed straight for the enemy lines. He nervously listened to the engine, haunted by the idea that a mechanical breakdown would mean a death sentence, because he would have to make a last-minute emergency landing. As he approached the Aisne river, the fog grew thicker and hung lower, as though it were pressing against the very ground, almost on a level with the pale outlines of the trenches.

Neuville turned to face Berthier, the crew commander, who smiled and pointed ahead.

Berthier was also agitated, but his was a different fear. He was worried they wouldn't fulfil their mission. Even though he'd been with the squadron for two years, he still felt as anxious as a rookie each time he flew. Better suited to dreaming and the pursuit of knowledge, he was afraid of being unable to grasp the true reality of things, and each time he climbed down from his cockpit, after having exhausted his pilot, he always had the feeling he'd forgotten some crucial detail. The idea of death and danger didn't affect him in the slightest, being so naive that he was utterly incapable of imagining his dreams might one day come to an end.

They were flying right over the front lines. There was a sort of sooty corridor between the layer of fog and the ground, which their biplane sped into at full speed. They were flying so close to the ground they could see the hollow casings and the tops of parapets.

"Fifteen metres at most," Neuville thought, clenching his teeth. "We've got to pull up."

Yet his skilled and experienced pilot's hand didn't budge and they headed straight into enemy territory. They reconnoitred the terrain over the entire front between Soissons and Reims in this manner without seeing anything. In the end, Berthier reluctantly gave Neuville the signal to head back to the base.

Thélis took great strides across the field, followed by Herbillon. The captain kept chewing on repressed expletives when a light suddenly made his face beam. A faint buzz, padded by the fog, could be heard coming from the direction of the Vesle river. The cadet couldn't distinguish it from the sound of the wind, but looking at Thélis, he realized that the plane was on its way back.

Marbot, Doc and all the comrades were already running over the field. The biplane burst through the mist.

"They're going to have a hard time landing," Thélis observed, still worried.

Yet on seeing how nimbly the plane was turning, and in awe of the pilot's artful manoeuvring, the captain was moved to exclaim: "That Neuville really is an ace pilot, what guts!"

By then the plane had landed and was rolling towards the hangar. Having reached the group of people waiting for him, Neuville climbed down from his cockpit. Berthier lingered in his, motionless. The captain shook him, laughing.

"Come on you dreamer!"

He stopped and raised the observer's face. His eyes were closed. There was a tear in his flight suit, close to the shoulder.

"Neuville!" Thélis cried. "Were you shot at from the ground?"

"I don't know, Captain, the engine was too loud for me to hear."

His voice was impassive, but he'd left his hood on so that his features could return to their usual coldness.

They carefully pulled Berthier out of his cockpit. His breathing was faint. Judging by the anxious faces surrounding him, Jean could see all the affection that Berthier inspired in the others. Doc unbuttoned his flight suit, then his jacket, examined the wound, and then stood back up.

"Well?" Thélis asked him.

"I'm not a doctor here, Captain, I'm just a pilot," Doc sternly replied. "We'll keep you posted once we get to the hospital."

Thélis didn't reply. Like everyone else, he'd already understood…

Jean couldn't help but think of the overflowing cheerfulness that had characterized the squadron less than an hour earlier.

So long as the fog persisted, there was no laughter in the mess hall. At the table, the greater amount of space between each place setting drew attention to the fact that one of them was missing. The absence was too loud. Yet by dint of their efforts to forget Berthier, his comrades succeeded.

Only Jean, whose sensitivity had meant those events had left a deeper impression on him, steadfastly refused to banish from his mind the memory of the only conversation he'd had with the deceased, or to forget the image of Berthier's face with his eyelids closed, his features already stiff, yet still sweet and pleasant. He'd wanted to talk about this with Thélis and Marbot, but they'd both refused him with such a tone that he couldn't have insisted. This seeming indifference would have shocked the young cadet if Captain Reuillard hadn't put it into a nutshell for him: "There's no point thinking about it, rookie," he said, "otherwise we wouldn't be able pluck up the courage to fly any more."

Amidst the silence that had deliberately erased the memory of their beloved comrade-in-arms, one could still sense a fighting instinct and a secret joy at still being alive.

When the west winds pushed the clouds past Reims, leaving a bright, spotless sky in its wake, this determination to forget asserted itself even more. Even though there were no missions at hand, other than the usual reconnaissance flights, Thélis ordered the entire squadron to take to the sky. Even Marbot, who tended to dislike flying when he didn't strictly need to, heartily approved of the captain's decision and said: "We have to wipe away all the bad memories."

The field was abuzz, a frenetic hive of activity. The captain was keeping an eye on everything: the engine tests, the departures, the landings and what the mechanics were up to. He told each pilot a joke. The captain's voice, which spread through everyone's nerves like wildfire, resounded everywhere. He kept running from the hangars to the planes, helping to start the propellers, checking the carburettors. Suddenly, as though intoxicated by the frenetic flurry he'd unleashed, he started rolling around on the grass with a beautiful golden retriever who never left his side and both lost themselves in their animalistic joy. Thus, he went from one plane to the next, spreading the fire that burned inside him, while each of the crews that were about to depart, to become a tiny spot in the vast expanse of the sky, felt the comradely passion that engulfed every fibre of the captain's being.

Herbillon went on his first flight that day. Evening was fast approaching by the time Thélis gave him the "go-ahead" gesture he'd been so anxiously awaiting. Afraid of anything that might delay his departure, Jean had brought all his equipment with him to the field early in the morning. He got ready so quickly that it brought a smile to the captain's lips and then he leaped into his cockpit.

Up until that point, Jean had only ever flown in training aeroplanes, slow machines that allowed one to see a landscape unfold, as though one were standing on a balcony. Yet now he felt a real warplane rumble beneath his feet. It was strong and swift, built for combat, a killing machine whose nose looked like a shark. Yet how narrow the cockpit where he'd inserted himself was, especially since a lot of the available space was taken up by the stool, the papers he'd brought with him and the butts of the twin machine guns! How could he possibly have enough room to carry out his observing duties and still fight at the same time?

The captain asked him if he was ready, and Jean bowed his head, feeling a mixture of sensuousness and anxiety course through his body. The plane began rolling bumpily across the field, then the shaking stopped and was replaced by a smooth, upward glide. Thanks to the brisk wind and the force of the propeller, the euphoria of the open skies washed over him, the same kind of intoxicating feeling sailors experience when they stand on the prow as their ship is about to depart.

The captain gained some altitude. At each turn, the horizon retreated further and further, while the land below faded away, and when the hangars were reduced to little more than white dots, Thélis pointed out the machine guns to Herbillon and motioned his hand towards the trigger. The cadet understood it was time to try out the weapons. He pressed his chest against the steel plate that welded the two barrels together and fired. A sharp, cheerful rattle rang out, disrupting the engine's rhythmic drone. Two red streaks flashed across the sky. The captain shouted enthusiastically: "Fireworks!"

He was answered by a fresh burst of gunfire, which startled him, but the song the bullets sang recalled the tune he'd been made to dance to in the mess hall. While testing his machine gun, Thélis had also started to hum the squadron's quadrille. The captain smiled at the cadet, filling the latter with a marvellous sense of happiness. Jean wanted to laugh, sing and cry. He admired himself: handsome, bold and serious as he set the infinite expanse of space on fire. He so dearly wished his mistress and all the young women in the world—all the women that his vague yet powerful desires led him towards—could see him now, in all of his angelic splendour. After all he'd read about aviators, and all the glorious halos he'd drawn above those pilots' heads during his long wait, Jean now had a halo of his own, which he wore like a crown of pride.

Without realizing which part of his exaltation was contrived, he leaned theatrically against the machine-gun turret and stroked the trigger with his furred glove. However, one quick glimpse below made him change his tune. The ground had completely vanished, and he couldn't make anything out any more. He feverishly tried to locate the white spots of the hangars, but all to no avail. Deprived of the only point of reference he'd had, he pulled out his map, which the wind almost ripped out of his hands.

He ducked his head inside the cockpit to examine the map, but immediately lost his bearings again as soon as he tried to apply the map to the landscape. He looked at the captain, as though asking for his help, but when he saw that his head was wrapped in fur and leather, he realized he was on his own, and that by the time they were in mid-air, the two metres of fuselage that separated them had become an unbridgeable distance.

Thus he decided to retain a visual memory of the shape of places while he flew above them so he could later put a name to them on his return.

Roads that looked as clear-cut as though they'd just been freshly painted coiled around the geometric shapes formed by the fields and woodlands. The villages looked like scatterings of tiny dice, topped by whimsical cones, while the rivers, which looked like motionless blue snakes, slumbered between the green lines.

Those were the trenches, laid out like a gigantic, fanciful chessboard, pale veins that had been sculpted into the same greyish soil where the river Aisne had carved its course. Tilting the plane, Thélis pointed out a snowy mass punctuated with shadowy lakes that could be seen through the wings' shrouds. Jean recognized it as Hill 108 because he'd seen pictures of that mound, which had been ripped apart when two trenches had been cut through it so that the French and the Germans could sit face to face and stare at each other. The plane had entered the undefinable no-man's-land that would soon lead into enemy territory.

Moved, Herbillon thought to himself: "We're going over to their side."

He steadied himself for battle, and thought he could see enemy planes coming from every direction, and mentally challenged them all.

Yet they were alone in that unblemished blue sky and, despite the engine's rumble, the young man could make out the silence unleashed by the twilight, which was starting to fill up the horizon. The sun was pink and the trenches had turned into bluish streams. The cathedral of Reims, surrounded by houses, was picking up the last glimmers of a sun that Herbillon could still see, even though it had disappeared out of sight for anyone standing on the ground.

Jean grew suddenly ashamed by the childish pride that had made him so fidgety. Now he felt very weak, very humble, and very small. The plane seemed puny to him, and he dreaded the terrible punishment that could be inflicted on those who dared to disturb the day in its mysterious death throes. He was knocked out of his reverie by a sudden bump. Thélis had started to nosedive towards the enemy trenches: a bloody spray of bullets burst out of his machine guns and disappeared into the bowels of the earth. Then Herbillon was hurled against his turret as Thélis pulled the plane up, like a rocket.

The young man's ears picked up a muffled sound, which seemed to dissolve in the air and he leaned over to try to hear it better. Under the fuselage, a curl of brown smoke had started to rise limply. Another rose on the left, and another still emerged from underneath the aircraft. They were all dense and mottled, like young trees in the springtime.

Thélis turned around to look at Herbillon and observe the effect that these first artillery shells had made on him. Had he trembled with fear, the officer cadet might have found some pride in smiling defiantly, but he didn't have the need to make such an effort. Far from frightening him, the explosions' suddenness had pleased him, as did the way they ebbed and flowed like languid waves, which made them look like little balloons that burst into grey filaments.

When the captain made an unconcerned gesture, Jean responded with a cheerful one, proud of how brave he was. Were those the dark clouds which the old pilots had spoken of with such dread? Yet they looked so graceful and made such a sweet noise! Could they really trouble a well-tempered heart?

Now he could see them everywhere: above, below, behind the plane and almost right in front of it. It was a kind of blossoming where one explosion would bloom and then fade away, only to start the cycle all over again, while the plane attempted to manoeuvre through that field of explosive flowers. Pitched on its side, the plane slipped between those smoky buoys, while Jean shook about, clinging to the edge of his cockpit, amused by what he thought was a game that Thélis was playing, not realizing that life and death hung in the balance.

The plane suddenly started to dance savagely. Despite the cadet's inexperience, he felt that this time it hadn't been the captain's doing. He didn't know quite how to explain that feeling, but he'd felt so carefree up until that point that it was only then that he realized he was sitting inside a lifeless machine, just a pile of wood, metal and canvas that had been assembled, and that he wasn't in fact sitting astride a docile, sensible beast as he'd previously thought.

At that moment, he remembered the earth. He looked at it, even though he was so distant and cut off from it, lost in a thin haze that was beginning to thicken. Jean experienced an acute desire to return to it.

CHAPTER III

AT THE SAME TIME, Deschamps was drinking with the NCOs as lazy words dropped from his lips while the others respectfully listened.

That mess hall, just like countless others, was furnished with a table and a bar. Yet everything looked as though it were of a lower quality, simpler, more neglected. Inside the barracks, the floorboards were loose, there were cigarette butts everywhere, and the air was thick and heavy. While the men, with their broad faces and dressed in coarse cloth, increasingly abandoned themselves to the flow of their emotions, finding it easier than usual to unwind.

There were three pilots there: Virense, a podgy, ruddy-faced boy, Brûlard, a former mechanic who'd become a pilot, and Laudet, whose grey hair framed his young features. Also present were Gival and Malote, the machine gunners, and Dufrêne, the photographer. Driven by Thélis's feverish enthusiasm, they had all flown that day, and the traces of that experience could still be detected in their eyes, which shone brighter.

While in their company, Deschamps came out of his shell. Up until his promotion to second lieutenant, which had only happened very recently, he had lived inside those barracks, eaten at that table, and drank the same viscous, bluish wine that now filled his glass. The day the squadron's tailor had sewn his officer's stripes to his peacoat had been the proudest of his life. It had fulfilled an ambition he'd secretly nourished, almost as though he'd been ashamed of it since it had always seemed too extravagant.

Yet once the initial euphoria had dissipated, his new status often got on his nerves, as though it trapped him like a uniform that was two sizes too small. At the officers' table, people spoke too meekly and their gestures were too restrained, and Deschamps was forced to keep an eye on his thick, calloused hands, which had been misshapen by working the fields and fighting in the war. Yearning for simplicity, and being all too rightly proud of his wounds and exploits, he was plagued by an inner turmoil that caused him endless suffering.

He only managed to feel like himself again when in the company of corporals and sergeants. When in their midst, he was a big fish in a small pond, the living embodiment of the honours and glories to which they could aspire, and since all of them knew the way he'd earned them, their admiration was fuelled by sheer envy. Of all the assembled men, Deschamps's old mechanic Brûlard was the most exhilarated.

A pilot entered the room and interrupted the conversation. Before speaking, he drained a large glass. "That's the stuff," he said, "after three hours of reconnaissance."

Virense asked: "Are there people still flying, Verraux?"

"The captain's still up there: I spotted him in the far distance out of the corner of my eye just as I was leaving."

He slowly removed his furs and the silk stocking he used as his balaclava, revealing his thin body, sleek hair and wet lips. His catlike movements betrayed the lover and prowler in him. Then he declared: "I saw a new face on the field."

He had enunciated each word so as to capture everyone's attention. Only Deschamps didn't turn his head.

"He's a lieutenant," Virense chimed in. "He started talking with Marbot when we landed. I think he's come to join our squadron."

Virense looked at Marbot, who was perfectly still, and asked him: "Do you know anything about this?"

A twitch on the mutilated man's face stretched his scar, but he coolly replied: "I've heard about him: Lieutenant Maury."

"It seems he's the new Chief Pilot," Verraux insisted.

This time, Deschamps couldn't contain his anger.

"That's right," he exclaimed, "and it's absolutely shameful: he's fresh out of school and just because he's got two stripes on his jacket they've put him in charge of people who've been through the thick of it!"

He struck his chest, making the medals that wouldn't leave him alone jingle in unison.

Brûlard stood up, and tremblingly fingered his raspy moustache.

"Are they going to do that to you, Louis?" he exclaimed.

"It's out of the captain's hands," Verraux bitterly noted. "The last orders were very clear: old pilots now have to be supervised by officers with two stripes."

"Let him try to give me an order," Laudet calmly said. "I'll throw a spanner in the works."

"As will I!" Brûlard exclaimed.

"I'll jam my machine guns!" Gival added.

"I'll do the same with the magazines!" Dufrêne concurred.

Deschamps happily listened to the brewing mutiny. He'd been appalled ever since he'd learned of the new officer's appointment a couple of days earlier. Being the captain's confidant, and as loyal to him as a dog and jealous as a wife, the news that an undeserving newcomer might come between them had dealt him a cruel blow.

"Let's go get a look at him," he suggested.

The bluish ashes of the evening rose in a luminous dusty cloud from the field, which was completely empty save for a mechanic shivering in the cold, waiting for Thélis's return. The pilots noticed a man pacing slowly next to the hangars with his head lowered. Despite his tall frame, he was stooping, and the snugness of his overcoat mercilessly sketched the outline of his gaunt, narrow torso and his slightly asymmetrical shoulders.

Having heard Deschamps and his comrades walk towards him, he approached them.

"Hello gentlemen," he exclaimed. "I'm Lieutenant Claude Maury."

He held out both his hands.

Leading the way, Deschamps merely raised his fingers to his kepi, and made no reply.

Maury's arms fell back alongside his body, inert. Faced with the hostility emanating from the group, he lingered hesitantly for a moment, disconcerted. He feverishly buttoned up his coat, vainly looking for something to say, or the right kind of attitude to adopt in response to their coldness. But an engine's murmur could be heard in the soft sky above, and everyone's eyes turned towards the foggy horizon where a plane's shape began to emerge…

The captain jumped from the plane and onto the field. Herbillon rushed to join him. The same emotions were written across both their faces.

"Well, rookie," Thélis said, "did you spot the battery that fired at us?"

"Not at all!" Jean cheerfully confessed.

"The little devil's doing well, just like I told you," Deschamps exclaimed, proudly showing off his intimacy with his commanding officer in front of the intruder.

Thélis had noticed the unfamiliar silhouette coming towards him and his features froze. He didn't want to let those jokes diminish his prestige in front of an officer whom he knew nothing about.

Herbillon didn't know whether he liked this new officer or whether he made him feel uneasy. Was he drawn to the new officer's thin mouth, which looked as though it had been painfully carved into his hairless cheeks? Or was it that broad, tall forehead marked by blue veins? Yet how could he possibly like his greyish pallor that seemed to spread under his skin, or the excessive gap between his nose and upper lip? And what about that clumsy body of his, the crooked knees, pelvis, shoulders—did it inspire pity or laughter?

Nevertheless, Maury brought the captain up to speed on his service record. Jean went to mingle with the pilots, who kept their penetrating, malicious gazes fixed on the new officer and followed the conversation. Jean could easily decipher the savage animosity in their faces, which looked impervious to any attempts to disarm it.

When Thélis led the officer cadet to the squadron's office so he could deliver his report, a shadow fell on the field, but it was still thin enough for him to distinguish a tall silhouette lingering immobile, like an abandoned wreck.

"What's changed here?" Jean thought to himself as he entered the mess hall. Neuville was rapping his fingers against a windowpane, Marbot was nibbling on his usual pipe, while Deschamps, Doc, Reuillard and the observers Charensole and Baissier were debating the merits of two different models of planes. Nothing seemed out of the ordinary.

Yet on noticing Maury alone in a corner, Jean understood that simply by virtue of having been excluded from the usual crowd, this new presence had disrupted the harmony.

Jean took his place behind the bar and asked: "Who's thirsty tonight?"

Maury started to approach him, hesitated, then addressed the rest of the room:

"Gentlemen," he said, "would you like to baptize my new presence among you?"

The phrase was too recherché, perhaps also too indirect?

Herbillon perceived the hesitation among the others, and then Deschamps brusquely declared: "Thanks, I don't drink."

The others reluctantly approached the bar, and all of a sudden Jean noticed Maury's narrow lips furtively but definitively bend into such a disconsolate frown, that Jean knew the embarrassment Maury had caused was making him suffer inordinately.

While preparing the drinks that had been ordered, Jean examined Maury. The small lines on his temples and his grey hair strongly marked the features of their new comrade, but he seemed especially weakened by an inner fatigue that appeared to make all his impulses powerless. When their gazes met, Maury's didn't shy away at all. Jean was the first to disengage, because Maury's gentle eyes were too easily penetrating his inner being and all too effortlessly overcoming the defences one raises against outsiders.

The alcohol that evening didn't do much to enliven the atmosphere. The insipid conversations dragged on and everyone waited on Captain Thélis to dispel the awkwardness. When Thélis finally appeared with all his sparkling personality, armed with the good cheer that always elevated him in the company of his comrades, even Maury himself smiled with relief.

He spontaneously asked: "So, how old are you, Captain?"

His voice betrayed a mixture of admiration and a kind of painful homage. However, nothing could have displeased Thélis more than a stranger reminding him of what he thought was his Achilles heel: his youth. He curtly replied: "Few of us aviators ever make it to old age."

By the sudden way Maury hung his head and lowered his gaze, one would have thought he'd been dealt a terrible blow. Yet he then mechanically directed his gaze towards the other officers in the room. Thélis was telling the truth: the oldest there wasn't even thirty years old. As though filled with shame, he touched his grey temples with his palm.

Jean had already started reading the menu out loud, peppering it with jokes and unpretentious rhymes. The captain, whose mood fluctuated like a child's, congratulated Jean on his efforts while laughing and affably motioned over to Maury to sit next to him, since he was the most senior officer there after him.

Before the dinner began, the waiters placed eight sealed bottles on the table.

"What's all this madness?" Thélis asked.

Seeing Jean's embarrassment, he added: "Was this you?"

"I took the liberty, Captain… to mark my first flight."

"Don't apologize, old chap, that would take the biscuit."

"Quite right," Marbot grumbled as he carefully uncorked the first bottle.

He dipped his lips into the dark wine and sighed: "Pity it's so expensive, I'd gladly drink it every day."

His sadness dissipated amidst the general laughter. Everyone cheerfully tucked into their meal. Maury felt a kind of primal brotherliness establish itself between him and his comrades, prompted by the warmth and the pleasures of the dinner table. The wine helped his greyish cheeks develop a little blush, and that faint glow helped dispel the distress in his eyes.

Thélis praised the squadron for all the spirit and enthusiasm they'd shown that day, but Marbot exclaimed: "Oh leave us alone! You were the first to leave and the last to come back!"

"He's right, Captain," Deschamps chimed in. "I don't like you being out there when it gets foggy. I'd be shitting my pants in your place."

On that note, Maury curiously turned to look at Deschamps, giving the latter the occasion to reveal the fury he'd been concealing.

"That's right, I'm scared, you heard me," he yelled. "Let's wait and see until you've accomplished as much as I have before you start judging me."

There was a great discomfort among all the assembled officers.

"Look," Claude muttered, "I didn't say anything at all."

Yet enraged by the reproach in everyone's eyes and drunk on both the wine and his resentments, Deschamps completely disregarded the reserve the captain expected everyone to keep while at the table. "I just wanted to make sure I pointed it out. Truly brave men don't think others are cowards."

Maury was frozen still. His lips trembled slightly at the corners. "I forbid you," he commanded in a soft, but steady voice, "to address me in that manner."

"Oh, *Mr Chief Pilot*…" Deschamps said mockingly.

A fist slammed down on the table loudly enough to make the windowpanes tremble and it completely silenced Deschamps. Captain Thélis stood up, having been lifted by such a wrath that everyone lowered their gaze in order to avoid his.

"Enough!" he yelled. "I don't want to hear any of these drunken quarrels. Deschamps, back to your room right now; you're confined until the morning. And as for you, Maury, as for you…" He waited until the disfigured man was out of sight and then he added: "As for you, well, nothing. You were right."

Claude stood up. "Captain," he said, "please allow me to withdraw. My trip here tired me out."

Thélis didn't hold him back. He secretly wished Maury had asked him to punish his best pilot.

Once the meal was over, Thélis, Neuville, Doc and Charensole went ahead with their daily game of bridge. Marbot began playing a game of solitaire. As for Baissier, he had a difficult monitoring mission ahead of him the next morning, and so he began to study some photographs.

Herbillon would usually stand behind the captain so the latter could teach him the subtleties of the game, but Jean was distracted that evening, and his thoughts lay with Lieutenant Maury.

Too few days had elapsed since his own arrival at the squadron for him to think unemotionally about the bare room where his new comrade was now holed up, nursing his sorrow, having been banished there by an inexplicable animosity towards him. Jean felt the need to go rescue him. Yet would such a move on his part wound a man who was older than him, as well as his superior officer? A sweet, cruel memory flashed across his mind and it ultimately forced his hand: that of Berthier coming into his room.

He found Claude on his bed, his body and hands completely limp. He must have just collapsed there and was lying there motionless. He didn't stir when the officer cadet walked in. It was only when Jean accidentally bumped into his trunk that the young officer raised his head.

The naked light bulb was emitting a harsh, blinding light that rebounded off the tarred paper walls, making them look even blacker. It fully revealed Maury's features, leaving not a single inch of flesh sheltered by the mercy of darkness. His face appeared drained by weariness.

Maury was aware of this and, with great effort, managed to show nothing more than some polite interest. Hesitantly, Herbillon started off the conversation: "Sorry to bother you," he said, "but I know just how disorientating it can be when you arrive here."

Jean didn't know how much sympathy he'd imparted with those words, and was surprised by the reaction they prompted. Maury stood to his feet, and grasping the young man's hands, he exclaimed: "How happy you've made me, my boy, how happy indeed!"

The officer cadet was lost for words. This man seemed to nurse a secret wound, which any carelessly uttered word might tear open again.

Claude began pacing around the room, making the kind of sudden gestures one might expect from a malfunctioning robot, thereby revealing all his body's defects. He visibly tried to control himself and begin a calm conversation, without, however, managing to do so. Finally, standing with his back to Jean, and with a voice that barely concealed its jitteriness, he asked: "So, what did I do to them?"

"Nothing, it's just a misunderstanding."

"No, no!" Maury exclaimed. "Deschamps hates me, and the others behave awkwardly around me, even the captain—"

"Don't speak ill of the captain," Jean quickly interjected. "You'll love him too, I'm sure of that, just wait until tomorrow."

Maury nodded his head and smiled: "But I love him already! He possesses a nobility of character that is indisputable; however, why—"

"Was he so curt with you?" Jean interrupted him. "You were wrong to ask him about his age."

"And yet I couldn't have paid him a bigger compliment," Maury declared.

He grasped the officer cadet's hands once more.

"There's nothing I find more admirable than youth, let me assure you," he added, his face overwhelmed by an absent gaze that revealed his obsessions, and as though a terrible doubt had just occurred to him, he added: "Nor is there anything more terrible."

His gaze came to rest on Jean's well-proportioned shoulders and tender features with a mixture of joy and an irrational fear.

"Did everyone here like you straight away?" he asked.

He realized he'd just embarrassed the young man and ran his long fingers against his forehead. "I'm incredibly sensitive this evening," he dully confessed. "Please don't judge me on the basis of what I've said. There are some days when one really feels one has reached the end of one's tether."

He began pacing around his room again, quickly exhausting its limited space with his long strides, once more searching for the right words to steer that strange conversation towards a more normal course. The officer cadet couldn't take his eyes off him, fascinated by his mechanical movements.

In the end, unable to put up with that seemingly unbreakable silence any longer, Herbillon made a suggestion: "Should we have a drink?"

Maury abruptly stopped, at first unable to understand what Jean had said. "But of course!" he exclaimed suddenly. "I should have offered you one right away. Please forgive me. What would you like?"

He started to fidget, trying to guess Jean's inclinations before the latter revealed them, but without letting him reply, he exclaimed: "Hang on! Perhaps you'd like some whisky? I've got some… they say it's quite excellent."

As the young man nodded his approval, Maury bent over one of his trunks and opened it energetically. Herbillon observed that the trunk was full of books.

Claude noticed his interest and, for the first time since he'd met him, the officer cadet saw Maury's lips form into a genuine, warm smile.

"I've got quite a few of them," he said, leaning on some covers.

Then he excitedly added: "They're at your disposal of course; please feel free to come in and take any of them whenever the fancy strikes you."

Herbillon nourished the kind of tenderness for books which, when shared, ensures a lifelong friendship. Maury divined his passion from the words the young man chose to thank him. Then, having both calmed down and begun to bond, they began examining the volumes.

Many of them were new and the pages were still uncut, but there were some used ones which indicated Maury's peculiar tastes. Claude explained his preferences, quoting some verses that Herbillon would then complete.

A deep-seated tenderness brought them closer together, while the wind outside began to blow with human cries.

Claude's eyes filled with gratitude and friendship for Herbillon. Having reached the bottom of his trunk, Claude then pulled out a sealed bottle, uncorked it, and filled two glasses to the brim. The officer cadet eyed his movements with unease.

"Do you want to send me on my way completely drunk?" he asked him.

Claude replied with a mixture of confusion and naivety. "I want to confess something to you," he said. "I've never drunk whisky in my life. I have no idea how much one should drink. But I want to become a true aviator, and drink and play with the best of them. You'll teach me all about that."

A twitch distorted his features. Jean couldn't tell whether he said the following either ironically or bitterly: "That's how we'll get women to like us, right?"

CHAPTER IV

THE MIST ENSURED Herbillon grew accustomed to lazy mornings. A vague sense of guilt struggled against a secret kind of pleasure, which Jean believed was closely related to cowardice. Yet what could he possibly do against a sky so pregnant with fog that it persisted in hovering above the ground almost level with the hangars themselves?

Jean's orderly went about his business inside the room. The water hummed while it boiled on the gas stove, and the young man listened to that noise, which had grown so familiar to him that he felt he'd been living his life according to its rhythm for years.

Jean got up late that day and, once he'd dressed, he headed to the mess hall where the officer responsible for the delivery of the mail usually left all the newspapers and letters. There were only three envelopes left on the table, and they were all addressed to him. He was surprised by how quickly he pounced on them. They were, after all, the same letters he was used to receiving, the same typically faithful missives he received from his parents, younger brother and Denise, and he was well acquainted with their affectionate, childish or passionate tones.

However, each line he read that morning insidiously prompted him to immediately—and despondently—reflect on what an insurmountable distance separated him from the people who had sent him those letters, despite their being only a few hours away, and whose tenderness he now beheld in his hands, if only for a moment.

Indulging his melancholy, he could now truly see his existence for what it was, which greatly differed from the heroic, unpredictable life he'd once pictured. Nothing could have been more monotonous and empty than those hours he spent shuffling around in clogs, immersed in gossip or playing cards, or the little walks he took between the barracks and the field, and from the field back to the barracks. Even his flights went by as regularly as any kind of office work, and most of them passed without incident. He muttered to himself: "It's like being sent into early retirement in the countryside."

He heard a comrade's footsteps and, as he feared revealing his weakness, he slipped the letters that were still in his hands into his breast pocket. Then, straightening up, he feigned a smile.

Maury wouldn't allow himself to be deceived. "You got the blues?" he asked affectionately.

His voice betrayed such concern that Jean didn't hesitate and confessed: "I feel pretty lonely this morning."

"Just this morning? You've been lucky."

Before replying to him, Jean looked at the empty table.

Jean then remembered the envelopes padding his peacoat and his fate instantly felt much sweeter. As Maury shyly asked him if he had seen any letters addressed to him, Jean couldn't help saying: "The last ones were for me."

The suffering he read on his comrade's features made him regret his words. To wipe it away, he added: "I'll take you to see Florence in Jonchery; we could do with the distraction."

They set off, on foot, down the plateau where the airfield was located, along the Vesle river, when an automobile stopped. Major Mercier, the division commander, offered to drive them. This completely dispelled Herbillon's unease. A courteous commander was driving them to an inn run by a beautiful girl.

Wasn't that enough to make one fall in love with life all over again?

The driver came to a stop in front of a low, small door. Claude and the officer cadet stepped inside the bar. The room's sole furnishings consisted of a bar counter and two long tables covered with a ragged wax-cloth with a few wobbly benches alongside them. As the room was dimly lit, they couldn't make out the silhouettes of the two men sitting at the back. Yet one of them stood up and they recognized him: it was NCO pilot Brûlard. Deschamps was smoking next to him.

Over the couple of weeks that had elapsed since their quarrel, Deschamps had come to appreciate Maury's reserve, and his initial hostility had melted away. Jean wanted to take advantage of the situation and definitively ensure their reconciliation. He took Claude by the arm and led him towards their comrades.

Deschamps affably said: "What are you drinking? Brûlard's buying, he's just been made sergeant."

Herbillon loved the bar's sad, seedy charm, its tangible warmth, the restfulness of the slouched bodies, the vacant minds and the simple gestures of pouring and drinking. Maury looked at him with astonishment. He just couldn't understand how that boy, whom he'd judged as sensitive and delicate, could possibly enjoy that smelly, shoddy-looking place, and the humdrum talk that filled it. Being there made Maury feel horribly embarrassed. Everything seemed hostile and repugnant to him, from the sticky lithographs hanging on the wall, to the red wine, which was wantonly consumed in big gulps.

Deschamps's cry worsened his unease: "Florence, at long last!"

A tall girl with painted lips appeared on the tavern's threshold, her pale-blonde locks having come undone after a run. Her full breasts, which huffed and puffed, jiggled inside her blue sweater and her incredibly short skirt revealed legs whose flesh could be seen through the holes in her badly mended silk stockings. She appeared to have been acquainted with Deschamps for quite some time and went to sit next to him.

Deschamps grabbed her by the back of the neck and drew her close to him. The rustic calm on his face had been replaced by primitive desire. His eyes shone with such a glow, and his lips began to twist so bluntly, that Maury turned away, as awkward as though he'd just seen a demonic apparition.

"I've got to write a report," he said. "I must get back."

Standing up too, Herbillon planted his lips in the warm nape of the girl's neck.

They walked in silence through the small city's streets, animated by the automobiles of the army's General Staff. Without looking directly at him, Maury asked Herbillon in a hushed tone: "How can you kiss a woman who belongs to another?"

"Come on, Deschamps isn't jealous of Florence!"

"I can believe that! But doesn't it disgust you a little?"

"Why? She has such wonderful skin…"

"So she belongs to everyone?"

"Just to me, for that moment."

"Well, isn't there a woman you love?" Maury asked.

"Of course."

Denise's charming ghost accompanied Jean on his walk through those muddy streets.

"Wouldn't it bother you," Claude continued, "to see another man caress her like that?"

Herbillon thought it over and exclaimed: "It really wouldn't, not at all."

A memory made him smile. Both to demonstrate the sincerity of his words, and to show off his conquests, he told Maury about his adventure on the train just a few moments after he'd left his mistress at the station.

Maury listened to him with a mixture of amazement and a confused sense of envy. How healthy that boy was, who knew of love only as a physical joy, and how innocently and naively proud of his good fortune he was! Nevertheless, Herbillon wanted to dispel the disapproval he felt his comrade nourished towards him. "Don't think I'm only capable of lust," he said. "There are different women for different emotions; some should only be desired, others should be treated with tenderness."

"Indeed," Maury pensively replied. "It's like Plato's old distinction between Celestial Aphrodite and Vulgar Aphrodite."

"Precisely, and both rule over me."

"Well, no, I can't go as far as that," Claude exclaimed. "Making the same gestures when they are unadorned by deeper feelings depletes the richness of the love which we are given."

A shudder ran through him and, suddenly sounding like an invalid obsessed with a fixed idea, in a way Herbillon had already heard him speak before, he said: "Do you think one can discern this kind of love in a woman?"

Without waiting for the officer cadet's reply, Maury continued in a hushed, mournful monotone: "I have a wife, she's young. She's my most prized book and also the longest: it's the book of my happiness. She's my gentle friend. But I've always lived on the margins of my desire. One might even say that the ability to adapt and the reflexes other people naturally possess are absent in me. I can't let myself go, and the same goes for my love. I desperately try to seek that spark in those cherished eyes, looking for that deep-seated vibration to reassure me, and I simply can't find it. I employ any means to try to awaken it, even the most ridiculous ones."

Their path began to rise steeply, while the wind lashed against their chests. He stopped so he could talk more quickly.

"Don't laugh! That's why I'm here among you. One day, when I had reached the end of my tether, a pilot came to see me. He was well groomed, his boots shone and, even to my cynical eyes, he had that mysterious prestige which all men with stripes on their jackets possess. Thus I thought I'd make myself more pleasing to women. But look at me. The uniform which hangs so well on you almost looks like a joke when I wear it. I've been here for fifteen days and I still haven't flown a single mission. My comrades didn't welcome me warmly and this morning, I didn't even get a letter."

By overemphasizing that last sentence and detaching it from the others, Maury had revealed the underlying reason behind his confidences, which, despite the fact he and Herbillon had grown closer and closer by the day, still shocked the officer cadet. So this was the mundane pain which that haughty forehead, so rich in subtlety of thought, concealed behind it! The young man's great friendship towards Maury was now intertwined with a little contempt. Jean still couldn't understand how anyone could suffer so much over a woman.

They started walking again. The wind was clearing the sky of clouds, sending them fleeing to the east in great hordes.

"So, tell me," Maury nervously asked, "is your mistress just as mysterious? Does she suddenly distance herself from you, fall into silences worse than arguments? Does her love ever seem to weaken, subdued by dark dreams? Do you ever catch a glimpse of intolerable pity or regret in her eyes?"

At which, in order to exact his revenge on Claude for his pressing line of questioning, as well as for the disappointment he'd caused him—and with the confused aim to show off the full extent of his happiness—Jean began to sketch a portrait of his relationship with Denise, matching Maury's descriptiveness.

He spoke of the unblemished joy of their rendezvous, their lighthearted cheerfulness, her vitality, her naive abandon and her boundless desire as she gave herself over to him. Each word made Maury sink further and further into his despair.

"Enough," he muttered. "It's useless, you're too young."

An automobile from the squadron caught up with them.

"Lieutenant," the driver told Maury, "the sky's brightened up, the captain is waiting for both you and Lieutenant Deschamps."

"He's with Florence," Jean exclaimed.

"I'll go fetch him."

Thélis had already had two pilots' outfits brought out. On spotting Maury, he cried from afar: "You're going to take me over the lines, Maury!"

Herbillon was bursting with admiration for the captain once again. While he always flew the inexperienced observers who'd just arrived at the front in his own plane in order to spare his other pilots the risk, he never entrusted their lives to a pilot unless he'd first put their technique and bravery to the test. Thus, he took upon himself all the dangers associated with those first few hours of flight, when the untrained eye failed to detect the deadly enemy before it was too late, or when awkward hands failed to handle both the plane and the machine gun.

"Go ahead and eat without us," Thélis said, turning to Jean, "and tell Deschamps to join us above the Chemin des Dames."

"You don't want me to fly with him, Captain?"

"No Mr Officer Cadet, Gival's going to partner up with him. You still haven't earned the right to fly with anyone except me."

The dinner had just begun when Deschamps came in, carrying his fur coat. "My blasted windmill won't be ready for another half-hour!" he furiously exclaimed.

He ate a little, muttering: "The Chemin des Dames is a bad area, the rookie won't know how to get back from there."

"Come now, relax," Marbot said. "Thélis has flown tougher missions than that."

"Sure, but he was the one handling the stick and rudder."

Impatient, he went out to the field. The sound of an engine's rumble above the mess hall told his comrades he'd left.

Once dinner was over, Marbot went to stand by the door and smoke his pipe, as usual. Old Captain Reuillard, who could not bend his memory to the whims of the Morse signal, went to sit next to the wireless. As for Neuville, Charensole and Doc, who were accustomed to playing bridge with Thélis, they asked Jean to sit in for him during his absence.

At that moment, Marbot called them. "Come look, Maury's back!"

"He's coming in at an odd angle, he cut the gas off too early."

The plane had begun its slow descent, bit by bit, as though the pilot was afraid of losing altitude too quickly.

"They must have suffered some kind of mechanical failure, for sure," Marbot said.

They burst into a joyous cry when they saw Thélis and Maury jump out of the plane after it landed. The captain was speaking excitedly.

"Good landing, but you went into a spiral dive too late back there; that's how they inflicted so much damage on us."

"You got shot at?" Marbot asked.

"Almost from the get-go," Thélis cheerfully answered, "we had four Fokkers on our tail; they shot a hole through our radiator. Fortunately we were flying at high altitudes, and so Maury brought us back down like a fine yachtsman."

"He got lucky," Herbillon said, "a dogfight on his first outing."

"Don't cry just yet young man," Marbot said. "You'll have your close shaves soon enough and you won't walk away feeling proud, let me assure you."

"Let's go eat," Thélis said. "I'm starving, and as for you lot…" But he stopped in his tracks. "Where's Deschamps?" he asked.

"He flew off to join you just a quarter of an hour ago because he had some engine trouble."

"He's going to come up against that flotilla of Fokkers. If it was anyone else I'd be worried, but he'll see himself through it."

Back in the mess hall, the captain saw that the cards had been dealt.

"Start the game—Herbillon, keep my seat warm for the time being and don't let me down!"

The officer cadet won the game and proudly informed Thélis, who stood up.

"Excellent my boy," he said. "Now let me put my luck to the test."

On taking his place he said: "Deschamps must still be looking for me out there."

While the game went on, Herbillon went to sit by Maury. "So, what did you think of your first fight?" he asked.

Claude was about to speak, but his lips formed into a tender smile and he muttered: "Forgive me for not telling you. There's someone I have to say it to first before I share it with anyone else."

Jean returned to the game of bridge. Thélis played his hand with the same glowing, childlike energy he applied to all his other pursuits, whether it was dancing the quadrille or fighting. As always, his ardour proved infectious and set the tone, and the game seemed all the livelier and appealing thanks to his presence.

Marbot, who'd been keeping watch by the door, interrupted them: "Hey, Thélis, Deschamps still hasn't returned."

A frown formed on the captain's brow, but he said: "He's been stuck here for a week, I bet he's just flying around."

Neuville was experiencing a bout of unbearable luck, and Thélis was hell-bent on defeating him. An hour went by quickly as they struggled. All of a sudden, the honey-coloured blanket that the sun had been casting on the table was replaced by a pallid curtain. Their eyes turned to the sky. Thick clouds obstructed it with their deathly pale flakes.

"Deschamps won't be long now," the captain said mechanically.

But he was surprised by the strange sound his voice had made. It betrayed a worry and anxiety he hadn't been conscious of until that moment, and which he could now see had spread to everyone else. Nevertheless, everyone tried to conceal it. Everyone in the squadron knew that talking about misfortunes was to encourage a self-fulfilling prophecy.

The game resumed, but everyone was irritated and afraid. Their fingers clutched the cards.

"You can't see anything out there," Doc suddenly said.

"Evening fell quickly," Herbillon commented.

"It's because we had a late lunch," Charensole observed.

They hung their heads to elude each others' gazes, if only to avoid their eyes expressing the thought that had flashed across all their minds. Everyone knew how

Deschamps loathed flying in the foggy twilight, and now they couldn't hear the noise of his plane, even from afar.

The silence was complete except for the noise Captain Reuillard made as he practised hitting the telegraph keys.

Turning to him, Thélis said: "Could you give it a rest, old chap? It sounds like you're typing out a distress call."

Then, addressing the players, he exclaimed: "Why are you all so quiet? We haven't finished. It's your hand, Doc!"

Their faces bent over their cards once again. In the meanwhile, the last burst of light outside had completely vanished. Large raindrops began striking the canvas roof like a gong.

"Come here, Herbillon," Thélis said.

Whispering in his ear, he told him: "I need you to place a call—not here, in the office—call the artillery batteries, the observers, the army corps, call everyone to see if there's any news."

By the time the young man returned, the light bulbs had been switched on. Even though Thélis didn't say anything, everyone turned to stare at Jean.

"Nobody knows anything," he said, making a gesture that unsuccessfully feigned indifference.

"There were four of them, right Thélis?" Marbot asked in a hushed tone.

The captain didn't answer him. Death entered the mess hall.

Invaded by that spectre, Neuville wanted a distraction. "Trump card," he said.

"Two clubs," Charensole replied.

The officer cadet felt that everyone was gasping for air, but he couldn't open the door because the night had turned stormy.

As they couldn't figure out what else to do, the game went on.

For the following two days in a row, they were besieged by a storm that confined them to their shaking barracks, while the winds howled their screams outside on the field. The gale tore the roofs off the hangars. In order to walk outside one had to struggle as though one were fighting a river's current.

Over those couple of days, Thélis kept waiting for news of Deschamps. He loved him deeply and passionately, perhaps in a less tender way than he'd loved Berthier, but his bond with the former was possibly stronger, since it had been forged through thousands of shared memories involving drinking sprees, reconnaissance missions and dogfights, all of which had been threaded together by three years of life in the squadron.

When he finally gave up all hope, he had the following sign hung in the mess hall:

A five-plane patrol at first light. To search for the fallen.

Marbot was the first to read the order and immediately went to look for Thélis. "You want to go avenge Deschamps, don't you?"

As the captain didn't reply, he carried on. "That's not our job. We're not fighter pilots."

"You're scared, eh Jelly?" Thélis spitefully retorted.

"You know full well that I always do my duty when called for," he said, "but you can't risk your skin—and ours—purely on the basis of emotions."

The captain's eyebrows twitched, but he restrained himself. "You're right," he observed. "I'll only ask for volunteers. But I'm telling you right now that I'm not taking you. I'll bring Herbillon with me since he's not too jaded."

"So you'll be crazy together. Goodnight."

Watching his thick silhouette try to negotiate the narrow door, Thélis shouted out: "Listen Marbot. You're right, but so am I. Isn't that what be both want?"

The large man gazed at him with his little, lively eyes. "My poor chap, you must really be agitated if you're apologizing to me."

He slapped the captain's shoulder, which was the most emotional gesture he could make. However, he still didn't offer to take part in the patrol.

The following morning, when his orderly came to wake him, Herbillon jumped out of bed with joy. This time he would finally fly *and* fight.

In his haste, he didn't bother to dress and simply slipped his furs over his pyjamas. He found Thélis in the mess hall: he was clean-shaven, powdered and groomed as though expected at a party. There was a plate of cold cuts and a bottle of rosé on the table.

A soft breeze, which still carried the fragrance and freshness of the night, wrapped itself around their foreheads. Outside, the first rays of light struggled against the darkness over the vast silence of the damp earth. Jean thought there could be no finer meal than those scraps of meat and that rugged wine, which he shared with his hero while waiting for the coming of day and glory.

Five planes were reverberating on the field. The engines' monstrous yell was scaring away the new morning's sweetness. The air whirled around them. The sky was as tender as a fragile flower that could only bathe for a few moments in the sun's youngest rays. The mechanics were singing and the propellers buzzed as though drunk on their own power.

Herbillon forgot about everything else as he savoured the pleasure that went with being strong and healthy, and flying into the blue at dawn.

The captain's plane was the first to reach high altitude, and Jean saw his comrades follow suit like brown rockets. Then the group headed towards enemy lines, having assumed a triangular formation.

The euphoria of flying was still new to Jean. The engine's gigantic breaths, the propeller's vortex, the furious winds, all combined into a vast, brutal symphony, which left him stunned. He'd barely begun to be able to distinguish all the instruments.

Soaring in such a manner into the solitude of the sky and seeing the red sun leap towards the horizon filled his chest with an unspeakable pride, as did the fact they were going to fight over enemy lines.

To complete his happiness, they would have to find

the fight the captain was looking for, hear the crackle of the machine guns and experience—and he was certain this was going to happen—the pride that comes with victory. He anxiously searched the sky in the hope of seeing planes with black crosses on their wings.

It was all in vain. They flew across the sky—which shone like a precious stone—for a long time, but saw nothing but emptiness. It seemed certain that this reconnaissance mission would pass without incident, dully, just like all his other missions before it.

To banish the disappointment from his thoughts, he absorbed himself in looking at the landscape, trying to unravel the tangle of trenches below, which the rising sun's oblique rays had turned into purplish streams. Yet Jean's still-inexperienced eyes failed to establish a fixed boundary between the opponents' lines and their own.

He worked at this fervently until a hard bump sent him crashing into the side of the cockpit. The plane nosedived, leaving a red trail in its wake.

"The captain must be a hot number in German trenches," he thought.

Meanwhile, the plane had taken a perpendicular angle, straightened out, gained new altitude with a brutal momentum, then nosedived again, sending Herbillon knocking around in all directions, bruising his shoulder against the gun turret.

Accustomed to Thélis taking those kinds of risks, the officer cadet peacefully put up with the aerial acrobatics.

The plane finally regained its balance and, turning towards Herbillon with a cheerful face, the captain pointed to a spot behind the biplane's tail.

Jean didn't notice anything aside from the fact that the other planes in their group had all vanished. He thought the captain was asking him whether he was afraid to continue the mission without their escort and so he made a gesture of indifference.

Nevertheless, their sudden disappearance left him feeling pensive.

"Maybe something happened to our comrades," he thought, "while the captain had his fun making me dance about inside the cockpit."

And, he concluded: "I'll have to ask him to stop joking around like that, he's getting in the way of my observing duties."

At that exact moment, Thélis sharply banked the plane, allowing Jean to see, far down below, a plane that was creeping towards the rear of the German front.

His heart skipped a beat. "A Fokker!"

Vigorously exerting himself, he swung his gun-turret around, and pointing his machine guns at the enemy plane, he fired. The bullets flew fairly close to the plane, but a new turn by Thélis removed the plane from his line of sight.

"If only he'd let me carry on," Jean thought, despairing, "I could have brought it down."

By the time the captain landed, three of the other planes were already on the field. As soon as they'd jumped out of their cockpits, Thélis turned to Herbillon and said: "Well, are you happy? You got the fight you were looking for?"

Thinking of the few bursts of gunfire he'd unleashed, Jean replied: "That wasn't a fight, it was nothing at all."

The captain looked at him with genuine admiration. "Congratulations rookie! Seven planes on our tails and we shot one of them down, but all of that isn't enough for you!"

A vague uneasiness crept into Jean's mind, which prevented him from speaking.

The captain really didn't seem like he was joking. Incidentally, the other crews drew near and the officer cadet heard Brûlard exclaim: "We got him, didn't we sir?"

"We did," Thélis yelled back. "Neuville and Virense shot it down."

Stunned, Herbillon hadn't quite grasped the extent of his misfortune. Far from being a prank, the captain's aerial acrobatics had been part of his manoeuvres during the dogfight—and while their comrades, who'd scattered during the attack, had been busy performing heroic feats, Jean had been busy studying the landscape, and, incapable of seeing those planes dance about, he'd missed the entire fight.

Shame swelled within him and made his cheeks blush, but as he still hadn't removed his balaclava, nobody noticed anything.

Overcoming his malaise, he was about to join the conversation when the last aircraft belonging to their patrol landed and rolled along the field. Doc sprang out of his cockpit and ran towards the assembled officers who were standing next to the hangars. His lips were contorted into a comical rage. As soon as he'd reached them, he yelled: "Which one of you beasts almost shot me down?"

Nobody answered, but Herbillon felt like he was about to faint. He couldn't even console himself with having at least frightened the enemy. He had shot at one of his own comrades.

Nevertheless, Captain Thélis pointed him out to everyone and said: “Our Herbillon’s got guts. We took a hard hit, and he didn’t even flinch.”

CHAPTER V

When Maury retired early to his room that evening after dinner, as per his custom, Thélis assembled all the observers in the mess hall.

"We must," he said, "replace the Deschamps-Gival crew. Only three of you are still unassigned: Reuillard, Charensole and Herbillon. Being new to their roles as pilots, Sergeant Duchêne and Corporal Boschot still aren't up to snuff. Maury, on the other hand, is worth as much as an old-timer. Who wants to fly with him? The most senior ones will have first pick of course."

Thélis looked at Reuillard, certain he'd happily pick the finest pilot, but the latter instead merely twirled his moustache to the point of almost tearing it out. Thélis's astonished gaze shifted from Reuillard's bony face to the others. He noticed the same hesitation on all their features.

Marbot, who was following the scene with interest, muttered: "They don't want to fly with him. He's jinxed!"

The captain let out a furious curse, but it was too late by then. The podgy lieutenant had perfectly encapsulated the observers' aversion, and fully aware of how superstitious his men were, since they put their lives at stake every day, he knew it would be difficult to find someone who would volunteer to share Maury's fate. Nevertheless, he kept trying.

"You're nothing but an idiot," he coolly told Marbot. "Maury's as good a pilot as I am and I envy his composure."

Nobody made an effort to reply, and Jean knew that the exact same ideas—which were incorrect yet highly persuasive—had settled into all of their minds. On his first flight, Maury had got into a dogfight and Deschamps had died trying to reach him.

This actually didn't stand up to any reasoning, but nobody wanted to admit it.

"I would prefer someone younger," Reuillard muttered. "Add both our ages and you get ninety years—that's a little heavy for such a little plane!"

"As for me," Charensole said, "I've already promised Boschot I'd fly with him: we're from the same regiment."

He was about to continue when Claude appeared.

Despite his usual ability to exercise self-restraint, Thélis couldn't help making a gesture towards his comrades.

Maury's sensitivity notwithstanding, it wasn't difficult to notice the awkwardness that his entry into the room had caused. It was so tangible that it physically oppressed him. As though to excuse himself, he hurriedly muttered: "I forgot my book on the table."

With everyone's eyes on him, he clumsily crossed the room, picked up his book, and then withdrew, walking in a more stooped fashion—and looking paler—than usual.

His sudden apparition did nothing to reassure the assembled men. How could anyone not link his fate to that body of his, which seemed to have already accepted its misfortune in advance? As struck as everyone else, Thélis couldn't figure out which line of argument to employ in order to continue the conversation.

At which point, Herbillon made his decision. While Maury's appearance had merely confirmed the others' doubts, it had actually reinforced the feeling of pity and respect that the young man felt for Claude. Perhaps all too vividly, Jean's imagination had pictured exactly the kind of distress his friend must have felt, having been rejected once again, in the cruellest of fashions, deprived of the comradely moral support he so desperately yearned for.

Needless to say, Maury wasn't exactly the kind of pilot Jean had dreamed would fly him to his most memorable missions. Yet his misadventure that morning counselled humility, and furthermore, wouldn't the fact he was volunteering for something everyone else was trying to avoid be the perfect means to show Captain Thélis how brave he was? Without knowing whether he was being prompted by vanity or compassion, Jean declared: "I'll join Maury's crew, Captain."

From that moment, on, Thélis addressed Jean by his first name.

Claude launched right into it as soon as the officer cadet entered his room. "So it's still going on," he railed. "Always the same hostility, the same unease."

Laughing, Herbillon said: "The unease will come later. For the time being, let's finish that whisky of yours, it seems I'm going to be your permanent passenger."

"What do you mean?"

"It's quite simple," Jean replied. "We're now a crew."

Claude's overbearingly penetrating eyes met with Jean's, and filling with boundless bitterness, Maury asked: "The others insisted on entrusting you to my care, didn't they?"

Then growing both tender and grave, as though about to swear an oath, he said: "They're right to do so."

Spring had triumphed. There was enthusiasm in the air, lights danced about, and from the heights achieved by the aeroplanes, the cathedral of Reims looked less discoloured. Claude and Jean flew many missions together.

Together, they experienced all the dawn departures, when the roaring engines stirred the day from its slumber; and the landings at sunset, when they cut out their engine, and slowly descended back to earth, keeping pace with the fading light. The unproblematic surveillance missions, the leisurely, watchful sorties; the dogfights where the mixture of hope and anxiety left a ringing in their ears. They shared the physical adrenaline of the sudden nosedives and the mathematical joys of aerial acrobatics. They learned to become simultaneously intuitive—as though by sheer, blind divination—of the enemy's approach. In the midst of the propeller's fury and winds that completely muffled human voices, they also learned to understand one another through gestures and signs. Maury, when turning around to look at his fellow crewman, would find his own thoughts mirrored in Jean's eyes.

They finally knew what their comrades meant by the word *crew*. They weren't simply two men flying on the same mission, exposing themselves to the same dangers, and reaping the same rewards. They were a moral entity, an organism with two hearts, two sets of instincts that governed a single rhythm. Their cohesiveness wasn't limited to the cockpit. It extended beyond it, by way of subtle antennae, by virtue of an irrepressible need to observe better and become better acquainted. All they had done was to learn to love one another; they completed one another.

Nevertheless, their habits and tastes didn't change. Their natures differed too greatly for that. Yet they were still linked by a mysterious harmony that was both invisible and unfailing, which, when they were flying through that crisp air—electrified with peril and euphoria—simultaneously stamped the same smile or frown on their mouths.

When the officer cadet was granted a period of leave from the front, Maury tasked him with delivering a letter to his wife.

PART TWO

CHAPTER I

THE DAY AFTER Herbillon's arrival in Paris proved to be quite bizarre.

Surrounded by his parents' joy and the sight of those dependable streets, with their familiar shapes and sounds, Jean was pursued by the faces of the men in his squadron. Thélis as he gave orders, Marbot as he smoked his pipe, or Maury's narrow neck as he bent over a book. The frail sunlight made him think about the fog hanging close to the ground, thwarting all observation efforts.

Nevertheless, he talked feverishly and voluminously, so as to satisfy the curiosity of the people around him. Yet a secret sense of disharmony prevented him from taking any pleasure in those conversations.

They expected him not only to regale them with stories, but to present them as though he'd written a book. Their imagination was wild as his own had been before he'd left for the front. It irked him to yield to the desire for amazing adventures that animated his interlocutors, and which forced him, despite himself, to paint a picture of life in the squadron. Would they really have believed him if he'd told them about all those lazy mornings and the mostly tranquil flights? The newspapers' pathetic penchant for exaggeration had too successfully bloated their imaginations for them to accept such simple, yet astonishing truths.

However, while he over-dramatized some events and underplayed others, he found himself obsessed by some seemingly unconnected words Maury had once uttered: "Do you know what a bayonet attack is? Cries, bodies swept along by an outside force, a terrible dryness in one's throat, that's all."

Nevertheless, by the time his first day back home had come to an end, giving Jean the time to became reacquainted with his old habits, the line demarcating his split personalities had become blurred once again. By the following day, when he welcomed Denise into his eager arms in his bachelor flat, Jean realized he was finally on holiday.

Jean hadn't initially recognized her thinned face. Judging by the way his heart leaped, he understood how much her body pleased him, and how much he cherished her flame-haired head.

They had exchanged a great many letters, but found they'd both changed in the interim. He'd been surprised to discover such an intense flavour on her lips, while she'd been astonished to see that only three months into his new life, Jean's still tender forehead now bore the marks of the tough decisions he'd had to make, and that there was a strange expression in his eyes, which differed from the childish gleam they'd possessed not all that long ago and made them look vaguer and sharper.

Denise pulled her loose locks up into a bun to get a better look at him. Beneath her gaze, Jean felt once more like the man he'd been when Denise had accompanied him to the station, an image of himself which his experience at the front had slowly withered. In her company, a naive sense of glory once more spread its wings, and when, in the midst of her embraces, he began recounting the tales of his flights and dogfights, embellishing them on an epic scale and peppering them with even more lies, this time Jean actually believed his own stories.

Their subsequent rendezvous were far less solemn. Picking up where they'd left off, their love affair resumed its usual lewd playfulness and cheerfulness.

Herbillon spent all his waking hours with Denise. She was always ready to meet him. He occasionally expressed his surprise at the complete freedom she enjoyed—while also choosing not to tamper with the mystery which he felt enveloped her life—but she would simply reply by way of a laugh, whose proud carefreeness revealed the monopoly that his tenderness exercised on her. Nevertheless, on those occasions, Jean thought he could perceive in her eyes a concern he'd never hitherto detected, as though she were repressing a question she didn't dare ask him…

One morning, Jean woke up to a feeling of regret. Amidst his confused thoughts, he remembered that his leave would come to an end the next day. This difficult realization came coupled with the memory of a duty which he had yet to fulfil. Day after day he'd repeatedly postponed delivering the letter Maury had entrusted to him, and it had lingered in his travel jacket for the past week.

He reproached himself sternly, and as he'd made plans with Denise that afternoon, he resolved to go to his friend's apartment that very morning, without any further delays.

All of a sudden, a curious sort of impatience took hold of him. He was finally going to meet the woman who'd filled Claude's life with passion and suffering.

Going on the portrait Maury had sketched for him, Jean envisioned a grave, pale face, a flat forehead and features loaded with mystery.

"Wouldn't it be funny if I fell in love with her?" he told himself with an incredulous smile.

He dressed himself with the most meticulous care, used a special kind of polish on his boots, which he looked after himself, put his kepi on his head with studied unkemptness, and went out, quite full of himself.

The maid invited him to wait, ushering him into a little drawing room. The curtains were cut from a very pale golden silk, which breathed a welcoming cheerfulness into the room. Large white vases were crowned with red marigolds. A low settee was covered with cushions upholstered in faded, precious cloths.

Herbillon was admiring his reflection in an oval-shaped mirror, which was framed in vintage silver, when the sound of brisk steps made his heart skip a beat. Before he'd had the time to understand why, a young woman had appeared on the threshold.

Jean let out a cry that he couldn't finish: "Den…"

He recognized his mistress, but encountering her there seemed so implausible that he initially doubted it was really her. She must have been her double, or maybe his eyes had grown so used to seeing Denise that he now saw her everywhere he went.

But the young woman lingered in the doorway and her voice—although it was barely audible—was precisely the one he was afraid he'd hear when she weakly said: "I've been waiting for you."

Herbillon slowly took some steps back, unable to tear his bewildered eyes off her. He was looking for a word or gesture that could pull him out of that dumbfounding reverie. Yet, while still lingering there, she carried on: "Claude has already written to me asking me whether you came by."

His friend's name on his mistress's lips. The letter in his pocket… Maury's confessions on the road back from Jonchery. Their embraces in his bachelor flat…

His brain was in a flurried turmoil. His limbs stiffened with a heavy torpor, and the sitting room around him became blurry. He stammered, as though to convince himself that the impossible had actually happened: "So… you're Hélène Maury."

She hung her head. Jean mopped his sweaty brow.

The young woman made a gesture of helplessness: it was all obviously clear. Nevertheless, she added: "I first realized it when I saw his address, then his letters confirmed that you'd been assigned to the same squadron. I thought you would have guessed the truth."

"What? You think I would have kept my mouth shut if I'd known?"

"I did what I thought was right!" she exclaimed.

She was animated by an unaccountable pride. In his anxiousness to understand the situation, Jean didn't take any heed of it. He confined himself to his own reasoning.

"How could I have guessed the truth? You kept everything from me: even your real name! Concealed everything down to the smallest detail!"

"But he must have spoken to you about me, I'm certain he did!" she exclaimed.

Her lover's eyes gazed at her as though he'd never seen her before. A stupefied murmur dropped from his lips: "Which eyes did he use to look at you? He must have described you a dozen times to me and I never had the slightest suspicion."

Overwhelmed, Jean thought about the monstrous mistake his friend had made, who still hadn't understood the fact that a woman could wear a hundred faces, and that all of them could be real, simply because they weren't conjured by that woman herself, but rather by the man who cherished her.

Taking advantage of his silence, she threw herself at him, wrapping her bare arms around him. "Kiss me, Jean," she pleaded.

Every single one of Jean's nerves rebelled. Denise had assumed that after the initial shock had worn away, he would take her back and things would carry on as usual. He harshly rejected her embrace and, employing a stern tone, he said: "Tell me, don't you know how much he loves you?"

Humiliation cast a shadow over her features, but she wanted his present refusal to have a flattering reason behind it. "Are you jealous?" she asked.

An insulting smile contorted Jean's face.

It was clear that Denise didn't want to grasp what a terrible disgrace this was, how it was on a par with suddenly revealing an act of incest, that Jean's feelings of pity and respect for Maury, along with their comradely fellowship, had been permanently corrupted and tarnished! And she'd dared to choose the very instant he'd learned the truth to try to tempt his body, whose stirring shape, which emerged from the half-open fabric, he'd turned away from with a strange sort of hatred.

Jean felt as though Maury's pitiful ghost was present in the room, observing their conversation, and every fibre of Jean's being trembled with furious indignation: his youthful sense of pride which still hadn't been corrupted by compromises, his instinct for camaraderie, which had been fuelled by life in the squadron, and the pride which he felt at being in the confidences of a man whose spiritual refinement was superior to his own, as well as his fiery nature, which refused to reach an accommodation with fate.

"Of course I'm jealous," he shouted. "But I would gladly take that a hundred, a thousand times over, you hear me! How am I supposed to go back there now?"

"Ah, so he's the one you're thinking about! I don't mean anything to you any more! So, you mean to tell me you didn't know I had a husband?"

Jean, in all sincerity, replied: "I didn't think he would be at the front."

"Why?"

"Because of his age."

"Why would you assume that?"

He was at a loss for a comeback. Triumphant, she continued: "So, having made an assumption which you didn't bother to verify, and which wouldn't have furthermore excused anything you've done, you've now completely absolved yourself, and you're going to blame me because fate put you in Claude's path?"

A sudden rush of anger made her neglect to pursue her advantage. "Why did he join the air force?" she shouted.

"Shut up!" Jean exclaimed. "It was to please you!"

"What an inspired choice!"

Jean couldn't understand that only a wild, boundless kind of love, which he was the recipient of, could possibly explain why Denise would rebel against a decision that would take him far away from her. Instead, he perceived it as cruelty, and it exasperated him.

"I really don't know who you are any more," he coolly told her.

"Of course, because you thought I was like you and that I was just playing at love, simply because I laughed to make you laugh, because I didn't want anything to darken your mood."

"Don't you get it? Your husband loves me like a brother!"

"You wouldn't think about that if you really loved me," she said in a hushed whisper as she collapsed onto the settee, exhausted.

Her anger had vanished. Tears brimmed in her eyes. Herbillon had never seen her cry before. He felt suddenly helpless, empty. Hadn't he been pointlessly brutal? What was she guilty of? He didn't know anything any more, save that his neck hurt and that he couldn't let that woman keep crying.

He planted a sweet kiss on her hair, then sat down beside her, helpless. They lingered there in silence for a long time. Denise awkwardly adjusted the bathrobe she was wearing, which had slipped slightly loose, revealing her neck. That shy, modest gesture, which was so alien to the mistress Jean had come to know, filled him with pity: for her, for Claude, and for himself.

Perceiving a poignant sorrow in his eyes, she said the following with an astonished pensiveness: "Do you really love him so much?"

He painfully hung his head, realizing she'd also submitted to Claude's invisible presence.

What could he possibly say to that? Of course, the feelings he had for Maury now bore no resemblance to the proud feeling of friendship he'd nursed for him before crossing that sitting room's threshold. It was now polluted by an aversion that had bent it out of shape, making it look grotesque. It was all so burdensome and intolerable that he stood up. Denise didn't try to hold him back.

"Are you leaving, Jean?" she asked him. And, after a long pause, she added: "Forever?"

He directed his lifeless eyes at her and replied: "I don't know."

He found himself back out in the street. The passers-by had translucent faces, and the cars wheeled along noiselessly. He couldn't hear anything except for the buzzing in his ears. He randomly walked into the thick throng of shadows to which he now also belonged.

However, a vague recollection made him quicken his pace. He had to dine early; he had to meet someone later that evening. But who? A powerful thought crossed his mind: Denise was waiting for him.

At that exact moment, all the street's noises, having been muted by some inexplicable spell, came pouring into his head. At the same time, all the men and women he crossed paths with on the streets had also reacquired their texture, while their skin once again bore the colour of live flesh. Being back among the living gave him such relief that the idea of seeing his mistress again soon actually seemed quite agreeable to him. He still imagined her as he'd seen her the previous day, when he'd been pleased by her carefree, graceful movements, and saw her smile, stretching out in ardent languor, admiring the blitheness of her grey eyes.

Jean's image of Denise suddenly seemed incredibly ancient, and the memory of the sitting room he'd just left rushed back. Instead of the face that it should have evoked, an anxious troubled face took its place, and the latter only bore a formal relationship to the former. He wanted to annihilate this new face. All to no avail, of course. The new vision supplanted the older one, and superimposed itself on it not like a mask, but like a living thing, albeit at first immobile. He realized he would never again find that face, which he had so long thought of as indelible and wholly his. Jean mused over how it had taken just a single morning to destroy a face even though it hadn't actually changed in the slightest.

On seeing him look so haggard and defeated, Jean's parents assumed that his sadness was caused by the thought of his imminent departure. In order to banish it, his parents feigned a cheerfulness which didn't actually brighten their eyes, while Jean, for his part, employed the same stratagem.

Nevertheless, the thought of how empty that afternoon ahead of him would be simply terrified him. He felt it would be impossible to sit down with a book. The enthralling hour when he could head to the bars was still some time away. His eyes met his younger brother's, which followed all his gestures with undying admiration.

"What are you doing after lunch, Georges?"

"I'm going to school, you know that!" he replied.

"No, you'll stay right here with me. We haven't had the chance to talk yet and I'm leaving tomorrow."

Jean knew his unexpected request couldn't be refused so long as he made it, and in order to replace that presence which had filled his days until that point, he needed the tenderness of a child who was entirely devoted to him, since it was almost as though Georges were in love with him.

Despite his father's protests, he took Georges to a café, ordered him liqueurs and treated him like a peer. He spoke to him of Thélis as though the captain were a legend, knowing that the boy would understand him better than anyone else. He asked Georges about his teachers and schoolmates. Hearing about his younger brother's life made him feel like himself again to the extent that he didn't need to fake his interest and the brothers laughed at the same jokes and were incensed by the same outrages.

By the time he took Georges back home, Jean's suffering had decreased. That childish exchange had lightened the heavy burden of his human pain.

Jean managed not to think about Denise a single time throughout the entire evening. He dined with old classmates of his from Fontainebleau who were also in town on leave. Coming from their camouflaged artillery batteries and their dugouts, they'd listened with admiration to Jean's stories about his life of freedom in the squadron, which was filled with comforts and risks. The thousands of creature comforts that Jean had looked on as insignificant over there, now acquired a great deal of importance when compared to the life led by his old classmates, and made him seem quite privileged. However, the daily, lethal risks he exposed himself to, which were the price he paid for those comforts, filled with him a secret disdain for those earthbound boys, or those "bookkeepers of bullets" as he called them in his head, the kind of soldiers whom pilots haughtily called *crawlers*.

Despite the police curfew, the dinner only drew to a close at six, with everyone drunk, as was to be expected.

However, the first image that flashed across Jean's still smoky mind was that of Denise. The argument which he'd successfully banished the previous day now came flooding back into his mind. He'd come to a decision as to how he would behave towards both Denise and Claude. He had plenty of time to decide what he would do with Claude, but, as for Denise, he felt forced to act without further delay.

They hadn't fully explained themselves to one another. Their last conversation had been marked by incoherent words and instinctive reactions. Could he truly break off a relationship while he was still under the effects of its poisonous charms? Why should he refuse to see her again and not tenderly confess his love, however impossible that love really was?

Yet, in a sudden about-face, the reasons that had seemed irrefutable just a moment earlier, now seemed powerless and, predicting Denise's responses, he felt completely disarmed, before he'd even begun. He could now consider this new situation from his mistress's perspective, rather than in terms of his relationship with Maury.

Truth be told, nothing had changed from Denise's point of view. What had been a heartbreaking revelation for Jean had been the mainstay of her life for the past several months. What could she have possibly done about the fact that her husband and her lover had been assigned to the same squadron, about the fact that they were now bound by a deep affection, about the fact that life in the squadron had soldered their nerves into a single body? Should she have pushed Jean away? How could she have shared the horror of a situation which she had accepted from the very start, and which Jean had remorselessly taken advantage of, even though he didn't even realize who the real victim was? Seeing as how he hadn't tried to understand her life, seeing as how he'd limited himself to taking pleasure in her body and her laughter, how could he then claim the right to insult her feelings, which he now realized were so alive and full of pain?

Despite realizing all this, Jean still couldn't go along with it. He knew this inner sense of conviction would prove stronger than all his other arguments. Consequently, due to his inability to prevail over his mistress, he resolved to leave without seeing Denise, regardless of the suffering it would cause him. He would only have to amuse himself for a few more hours before life in the squadron completely absorbed him once again.

He spent the last day in his family's company, steeped in the languid sadness that follows in the wake of all renunciations. Yet while they spoke softly amidst the falling shadows, the spectre of death glided towards Herbillon. Some of his comrades' phrases resounded in his memory: "One squadron can always be replaced by another." "The more you fly, the unluckier you get."

Over the course of just a few weeks—and during a lull in the fighting to boot—he had witnessed the deaths of Berthier, Deschamps and Gival. Nothing justified his faith in his body's invulnerability. A single burst from one of those artillery shells that peppered his aerial path was enough to make him shut his eyes in fear. His fate hinged on the skill of a German fighter pilot, or the trajectory of a bullet—which usually hit its target merely by happen-chance—or on an engine's badly timed tantrum.

How fragile his life really was—and how shallow the anguish which had gripped him over the past couple of days! How brittle his chances—and Maury's—were when it came to escaping all the pitfalls that lurked in the skies. Furthermore, wouldn't their simultaneous demise soon resolve the entire matter anyway?

At which point, Jean's breast swelled with a desire as deeply rooted as his will to live. Since all the above-mentioned was true, and that nothing truly mattered when death was constantly snapping at his heels, didn't he have a right to have everything he wanted? Why should he refuse the ultimate gift that destiny had offered him?

Night fell, sparking the fire of desire. Denise was luring him towards that house whose existence he'd been completely oblivious to until the previous day. Jean made his way over there, haunted only by the fear that he wouldn't find her there.

When she noticed his feverish eyes and his trembling lips, she threw herself at him, more passionate and beautiful than ever before.

CHAPTER II

THE TRAIN WAS conveying Herbillon to the front once again. Yet his thoughts lay with the first train he'd travelled on three months earlier, a time he now looked on both tenderly and condescendingly, as one behaves towards a sibling who's both a lot younger and infinitely less worldly.

This time, Jean's impatience to reach the front didn't seize his throat with an intoxicating anxiety. The questions which had seemed so essential prior to his first departure no longer mattered. Now he knew that one couldn't impress anyone at the squadron by dint of one's courage, because, brave or not, everyone genuinely set themselves to the same dangerous tasks. Now he knew that the art of looking was more highly prized than recklessness, that the whimsical path of a stray bullet could lead one to victory just as much as a martyr's death, and that luck ultimately determined one's achievements in life. This luck, which he could only observe like a passive bystander, also inspired a fear which he was no longer ashamed of, now that he knew he could pull himself together while seated in his cockpit, able to muster all his sangfroid and determination he would need to succeed.

He allowed himself to bounce about on his seat without any melancholy. If his experiences thus far had stripped him of his heroic illusions, it had replaced them with a practicality that provided him with some comfort. Once he arrived at the station in Jonchery, he waited for the car emblazoned with the White Rabbit, the squadron's mascot. Back in his familiar room where, thanks to his efforts, the walls no longer looked so sullen, Mathieu the orderly had lit the gas stove and unleashed its crackling song. On waking the next morning, Jean would meet up with his comrades once again. Thélis's laughter would animate the mess hall; Marbot's delighted face would be astonished by all the money Jean had spent during his leave; while Captain Reuillard, with his grey moustache, would make some obscene comment or other.

Jean had returned to the fold of his large, welcoming family, the wholesome, coarse clan of men whose existences were governed by basic laws that didn't burden them with unnecessary worries.

As he'd drawn towards the end of his journey, the images of Paris, which he'd lived so vividly until only a few hours earlier, began to fade until they completely vanished.

It had taken him a day to adapt back to life as a civilian, but the front had reabsorbed him before he'd even returned to it.

The following day, while the first few moments that followed sleep still kept the officer cadet glued to the web of his dreams, Maury cautiously entered his room. Herbillon shut his eyes in a subconsciously defensive manner, but he still observed Claude through his half-shut lids.

Claude had stopped on the threshold. His pensive head, which poked out of the dressing gown that concealed his body's defects, was ennobled by the morning's light. He gazed at Herbillon for a long time. His face, which was unaware it was being observed, was marked by a friendship that was so deep and generous that the officer cadet found the sight of it unbearable. His regrets, which had faded away when he'd shared his last embrace with his mistress, now re-emerged, sharper than ever. Jean wanted to shout: "You can't look at me like that any more!"

But Maury shyly shut the door.

As soon as he did so, Jean reopened his lucid eyes to reality. He couldn't even claim ignorance as an excuse any more, because before leaving Paris he'd committed the ultimate act of betrayal. The sophistry he'd used to distract himself crumbled away in that cold room, which was as austere as a monk's cell. Everything was clear-cut here, just like life in the squadron, and this forced him to judge things with unsparing clarity. The situation which had seemed so complex in Paris now seemed so straightforward.

The young man firmly resolved to beg the captain to bring his partnership with Maury to an end and, if necessary, to come clean with Claude about everything. It was the only way he could behave with dignity, and there was a chance Claude might even forgive him.

He self-righteously pictured that scene, where both parties spoke honestly and candidly, while respecting each others' dignity, and Jean thought that it would play out in a manner that would be in keeping with the life he'd just resumed. Unable to consider how that scene might also play out in a childish, cruel and even pathetic way, he rose out of bed feeling relieved and overjoyed to see his comrades again.

The reception he received was exactly the one he'd expected. In the time that had elapsed since his first arrival, he had simply become someone who'd come to reclaim his place at the table and play his part in the common fight. His comrades introduced him to the latest arrivals: Narbonne, who had replaced Deschamps, and the cadet-observer Michel. Jean learned that Neuville had been awarded the Croix de Guerre, and then almost immediately recalled back to the Ministry, that Brûlard had been wounded in action and that Florence in Jonchery was suspected of espionage.

The day went by quickly, to the rhythm of the usual habits which Jean self-satisfyingly slid back into by rote. He arranged some new fabrics in his room which he'd purchased while on leave, unpacked some books, went out to the field, paid a visit to the NCOs, and settled back into the life he would lead for the next four months: that is unless an accident—which was highly likely, despite his refusal to admit it—put an early end to it.

When Jean, wearing his clogs, worn-out sweater and an old jacket, went to lean on the bar, which was being tended to by the new rookie, his first conversation with Marbot came flooding back into his mind, and he admitted that the pudgy observer had been right all along. What really mattered at the squadron wasn't how many missions one flew, nor one's acts of bravery, fear, nor even the deaths: it was comforts, and the art of making them happen.

While Jean was smoking with a glass of port in front of him, a familiarly nervous hand touched him.

"You're drinking on your own, my unkind crewman, you haven't yet found a moment to speak with me," Maury exclaimed.

Herbillon made a vague gesture, but his friend's remark filled him with shame. He had in fact avoided being alone with Maury at all costs, and this seemed to him strikingly cowardly. Seeing how Jean owed him a clear-cut explanation, why was he going about it so poorly?

Jean answered: "I'll postpone our conversation to this evening."

His voice betrayed the effort that enduring Maury's gaze cost him, as well as the grave, sombre task he'd settled on accomplishing. Maury noticed all this but, being well aware of how unhealthily obsessive and occasionally misleading his sensitivity could be, he refused to pay it any heed.

Some of their comrades entered the mess hall, bringing with them that unfussy cheerfulness that characterized that large room which housed the squadron's sonorous soul. Assailed by jokes on all sides, Jean turned away from Maury.

Once the table had been cleared, Thélis asked him: "Are you going to play bridge with us tonight, Jean?"

The officer cadet hesitated. Maury had directed his supplicating gaze towards him. Was he going to further delay the hour of his confession? Already gladdened by the prospect of yet another deferral, Jean didn't want to give in to his weakness.

"Not tonight, Captain, I'm going to turn in early."

His response prompted a number of flattering taunts about how he'd spent his time on leave, but Jean had in the meanwhile already started walking down the corridor.

Despite Claude's impatience, which Jean had tremblingly guessed, the former didn't say a word until they'd reached Claude's room, as though he couldn't bear the idea of confessing his emotions outside unfamiliar walls. However, as soon as the door had shut behind them, and before the officer cadet had had the chance to compose himself and steel his resolve, Maury asked him: "So, what did you think of Hélène? Did she talk about me a lot?"

Faced with Maury's wide eyes, and that tense body of his, which was so frail that a carelessly placed word might shatter it at any moment, the young man thought he would never muster the impossible strength he would need to speak. His voice was refusing to utter the words that had sounded so noble and natural when he'd been on his own. No, in the face of such love it was better to lie, to lie with tenacity, guile and perseverance, to lie like a desperate woman, rather than let the truth leak out drop by drop.

He suddenly realized how impalpable those long silences were, which he'd previously looked on ignominiously. Jean's heart filled with immense contempt and a bitter sadness at life as he began to talk verbosely about Madame Maury's virtues and the love she bore her husband, his mannerisms betraying an angry, almost intoxicated kind of self-loathing.

When he'd finished, Claude's attentive gaze was full of surprise. "She really loves me?" he asked.

"It's just like I've told you," Jean exclaimed.

Claude was struck by the harshness of Jean's tone, and he realized that the officer cadet's words hadn't filled him with joy in the way he'd rightfully expected them to. Jean detected a strange disbelief taking root in Claude.

While they couldn't truly glimpse into each other's emotions, those hours spent flying together hadn't been in vain since they had given them the secret power of mutual insights.

Almost absent-mindedly, Claude murmured: "You're not keeping anything from me?"

Herbillon was seized by a furious desire to come clean. It was too late: his absolute certainty that he lacked the necessary strength to speak candidly to Claude had already taken hold.

"So your unhealthy scepticism extends to me too?" he asked, forcing a smile.

No other line of argument would have worked. Yet Claude held Herbillon's honesty and friendship in such high regard that he was suddenly cheerful again.

"Now, why don't you tell me about *your* friend?" he asked affectionately.

Jean stood up abruptly. He had been able to construct a vague, abstract portrait of Hélène Maury in his remarks, yet juxtaposing it with the image of Denise, which was still so alive—and warm with betrayal and lust—was completely beyond his powers.

"Forgive me," he said, "I'm truly exhausted."

He rushed out of the room, and Maury felt suddenly cold.

CHAPTER III

"WE NEED ANOTHER place setting!" Herbillon shouted.

Officer cadet Michel, his junior, who was setting the table, continued to arrange the champagne glasses.

"A special guest?" Jean asked him.

"Captain's orders. I don't know anything," Michel answered.

"So let's have a glass while we wait."

They drank and Michel asked: "Do you want to know the reason behind all this fuss?"

"But you don't know either."

"Not at all, it's just that Thélis ordered me to keep my mouth shut."

"A surprise?"

"For some."

A shy silhouette filled the door frame; a southern accent greeted the young men. It was Virense. "The captain asked for me," he said.

"You're dining with us," Michel answered.

Herbillon and the pilot looked at him with the same astonishment. The NCOs always ate in their own mess hall. Nevertheless, Michel carried on, impassively: "The captain recommended I double the portions. It appears you've got a robust stomach, old chap."

Having just entered the room, Thélis overheard him. "Leave that boy alone," he exclaimed. "Virense is like a rosy-cheeked girl. Pour us some port in some large glasses. Herbillon's buying."

"You've been running around mysteriously all morning, Captain," the young man said.

Thélis made no reply other than to slap his shoulder. The room gradually filled up and Jean thought he could detect a cheerful conspiracy on all the assembled faces, except for Claude's, which was still missing.

"Let's have a proper quadrille!" Thélis exclaimed.

While the burlesque rhythm made the boots and clogs pound the floorboards, Jean reminisced about the first dance he'd seen on his arrival. Half of the people present in the room at the time were gone. This realization dawned on him without any melancholy. Quite the contrary, it actually allowed him to savour the happiness that enlivened all those bodies all the more, and since Marbot was begging for mercy, having run out of breath, Jean called for another dance.

Then the meal began. It was the hour when everyone loved one another. Having left the dangerous skies behind them, the airmen, with their shiny teeth, healthy appetites and merry sounds, had brought back a hunger for food and laughter, a need for friendship, and a hearty zest for life that infected everyone at the table with happiness while they feasted and yelled.

The captain sat Virense next to him and placed Maury, who was now the most senior pilot, next to Herbillon. The squadron's cellars had a few fine vintages in store. Thélis ordered them to be brought up, one by one.

"So who do we owe all this to?" Jean asked.

"Drink!" was the only answer he obtained.

Glasses were drained amidst all the hubbub. The alcohol kindled the usual cheer. Jean felt as though everyone was looking at him, Claude and Virense with a sardonic tenderness. This intrigued him because he couldn't help himself from thinking that Thélis had planned some big practical joke at his expense, but all the cries, wine and cheerfulness, all of which were even more exhilarated than usual, left him neither the time nor the means to try to guess what was going on.

When the bubbling champagne had filled the cups, the cacophony suddenly died. Everyone's eyes turned to the captain, who stood up and exclaimed: "Maury, Herbillon, Virense, come here, and bring your glasses."

They obeyed.

"Let's drink," Thélis said.

Setting his drained cup down on the table, Thélis pulled three sheets of paper out of his pocket, picked one out randomly and read it out loud:

"Army Corps Citation: Officer Cadet Observer Jean Pierre Herbillon, Squadron 39. On 15 March, under heavy fire from anti-aircraft artillery batteries, successfully photographed a target. On 26 March, together with his pilot, he shot down a Drachen. On 2 April, he was attacked by two fighters, repelled their offensive and successfully carried out his mission."

Thélis had barely finished reading the sheet when Marbot yelled out: "Come on you lot, let's have a round of applause, and let's bring the roof down!"

While the crockery and dinnerware clanged, the captain clumsily pinned the Croix onto Jean's jacket, pricking him painfully on his chest as he did so, prompting Jean to think: "This is the most pain I've felt throughout the entire process."

Thélis then began reading out Virense's citation and Jean sat back down. In a state of torpor, he looked on as his comrades came to clink their cups against his. He replied to their congratulations mechanically, as though completely detached from the friendly group of men around him, isolated by a strange feeling of loneliness.

So this was what he'd dreamed of—what a wonderful reward! This was what he had looked on with religious desire when he'd seen it pinned to other people's uniforms! Yet now that Thélis, whom he idolized and was his commanding officer, had just pinned the same medal to his chest, Jean felt no excitement or pride whatsoever! Had the surprise killed the joy even though it should have increased it?

A moment's self-reflection provided him with the reason for his astonishing indifference: he hadn't deserved that Croix in the slightest, or at least he hadn't accomplished anything spectacular enough to earn it. He remembered the words of the citation. Of course, they were based on real events, but they presumed that he'd played a decisive role, and that he'd made an active display of courage when he actually hadn't. After he'd weighed these thoughts, he felt like a fraud.

He had successfully photographed a target when he'd been wrapped in such thick black smoke that he could have almost touched it, but it had all seemed so harmless that he hadn't even been bothered by it. He and Maury had indeed shot down a Drachen balloon, but the sky at the time had been so devoid of enemy aircraft that it had felt like target practice. He had also been shot at by two German fighter planes, but they'd missed so spectacularly that they'd probably given up the chase in frustration, thus allowing him to complete his reconnaissance mission.

On each of those occasions, Jean had been impervious to fear, and had shrugged those shells and bullets off, but each and every one of his comrades along that vast front had done the exact same thing whenever they'd gone out on their own missions. Thus, on that basis, shouldn't everyone get a medal every day for their own efforts? What unique, worthy feat had he achieved? What striking act had he been singled out for? He turned his anxious eyes towards those familiar faces, searching for an explanation, and yet saw nothing but calm affection in them.

At that moment, Claude returned to his seat with his own medal, and Jean detected the same painful indifference in the latter's features. Jean thought to himself: "He doesn't know either."

He had never felt as close to Claude since his return from Paris as he did then, nor as powerless to confide in him. Noticing this, Maury hoped that this incomprehensible awkwardness, which had grown more intense with each passing day, might finally melt away on this occasion, when they had brought honour and acclaim to their squadron in the presence of their assembled comrades.

"The only worth I attach to this medal," he said in a hushed whisper, "is that I received it beside you."

Before the young man could reply, Thélis shouted: "Maury, Herbillon! Have you no shame? You forgot to make a toast! Besides, when crewmen are awarded a medal together they're also expected to hug!"

Maury leaned towards Herbillon, every fibre of his lanky, sickly being pulsing with friendship for Herbillon. Yet the young man didn't budge an inch.

Even if he'd wanted to, the gesture Thélis had called for was simply impossible. His arms refused to obey him. He would not give Maury that Judas kiss while the captain and his comrades looked on. He wouldn't allow his cowardice to stoop so low.

"Are you awake?" Thélis asked.

Herbillon stubbornly kept his gaze fixed on the table.

But Claude had arched his back away, avoiding contact with the young man. Forcing a smile, he said: "Please don't insist, Captain. Jean hates public displays of affection."

"My word! The boy's crazy!" Thélis mumbled.

Then, noticing the awkwardness the incident had created, he exclaimed: "The meeting's adjourned! Now who's going to come with me to the new battery of the 105?"

"I will," Jean exclaimed, the fear of being left alone with Maury dispelling his dreadful torpor.

"So the baby's finally woken up! So the baby wants to show off his medal to the artillerymen. Fine, since I can't refuse you anything today, I'll take you there."

Having thrown a goatskin over his shoulders, Jean sat next to Thélis.

"Keep your cool," the captain told him. "I'm more dangerous behind the wheel of a car than when I'm flying." The violent air closed in around them, while the car danced along the potholed road. Speed, which always left Jean feeling intoxicated, chased his troubled memories and regrets away. As always, Thélis's *joie de vivre* proved infectious.

Experiencing a bizarre change in mood, Jean was finally able to savour the pleasure of having been awarded a medal. His imagination, which enjoyed conjuring theatrical visions, painted that crazy car race—where the two brave, young, elegant pilots raced towards the front—in the most glorious of colours. To ensure others would see it, he puffed up his chest to proudly display where his medal was pinned.

Paying no heed to the craters hollowed out by the shells, the rickety bridges and the deadly twists and turns, the captain pushed the car's engine to the limits. Jonchery, which still clung to life, and Cormicy, which had been completely destroyed, faded fast in the distance. Once they reached a crossroads, Herbillon went hurtling against the windscreen. Thélis hit the brakes.

An arrhythmic stomping animated the camouflaged path that led to the nearby trenches.

"The next shift," the captain said.

The soldiers slowly trudged past them. Their misshapen boots were barely touching the hard ground. Their backs were bent under the weight of their equipment.

Every single one of their faces, no matter how different, all bore the same expression, one might even say the same grisly, brotherly make-up. The same huge eyes poked out of the same scraggly beards that made their skin itch.

Herbillon saw them cast jealous, hateful glances at their car, their fur coats, and their calm, well-fed, well-groomed faces. He spared a quick thought to the meal he'd just consumed, and all that champagne… Afraid that Thélis would notice him, Jean imperceptibly moved his clenched hand and covered up his new, shiny medal.

CHAPTER IV

THEY SIMULTANEOUSLY jumped out of the plane, which had come to a halt next to the hangars. Seeing their bodies shake from head to toe, in such a way that even the safety of the hard ground beneath their feet didn't quite dispel, Marbot immediately understood what had happened.

"You took a hard hit?" he asked.

"This time I really think I got scared," Herbillon said.

"Nothing to brag about," the fat man calmly muttered.

Jean and Maury started speaking simultaneously. They'd been surprised by the arrival of two fighter planes that had proven uniquely skilled and tenacious. Claude's machine gun had jammed on a bullet, while Jean's had been useless since the planes kept flying underneath them. Both had heard the red-hot bullets whistle past them and it had been a sheer miracle that they hadn't caught fire.

Marbot approached their plane.

"You got a nice skimming ladle there," he remarked. "Twenty-eight holes in the fuselage."

"My arm's sore," Maury suddenly said.

Herbillon wanted to help him out of his flight suit, but hesitated. The sleeve was torn in the spot Claude had pointed out and there was a patch of bloodied fur.

"The bullet's fiery gust grazed past you and wounded you," Jean said.

"Same goes for you," Marbot remarked, "I can see through your sweater."

Jean looked down at this torso. His jacket and sweater had been torn in seven different places.

He breathed deeply, greedily sucking the air into his lungs. Claude had the same reflex. They looked at one another with the same hallucinated stare in their eyes. The terrible tension that had fused their individual fears and hopes into a single alloy persisted within them. They thought that one's gesture should automatically inspire a complementary reaction in the other. The danger they'd just evaded, which had been more critical than any they'd hitherto experienced, had brought them together to an even greater extent.

"How did this happen, were you half-asleep?" Marbot exclaimed. "I thought both of you had a good eye."

Their gazes met once more, but this time they both turned away. The dream they'd chased up there, under that pale sky, had come back to haunt them once the first shots had crackled and whizzed past them.

Maury thought: "Why have Hélène's letters betrayed a great deal of anxiety ever since Herbillon's return, and why is he so different now?"

While Jean thought: "Does Claude already suspect me?"

They were in the grips of the fear that often dulled their senses and attention spans after hours of flying. However, how could they possibly confess that to Marbot? They both replied to his questions in a vaguely dismissive manner.

They headed back to their barracks, exchanging the usual reflections on the fight they'd just been through. The emotions that had electrified their bodies wasn't fading away. Yet far from easing the awkwardness they felt in each others' company, their quasi-mechanical kinship actually increased their unease, because it allowed them to glimpse into each others' souls, threatening to expose everything they wanted to conceal.

It was the hour when the mail was delivered. The envelopes' bright colours decorated the tables in the mess hall. Standing at the door, they could already see which ones belonged to them, and Herbillon tightly clenched his jaws to conceal the turmoil he was in. There were two letters from Denise—almost side by side—one for him, and one for Claude. Even though Jean's was in a different envelope and Denise had tried to camouflage her handwriting, Jean thought Maury wouldn't be so easily deceived. He sped past his comrade and rushed towards the table. Seizing the letter in his hand, he exclaimed: "It's a pleasure to see this after the danger we've been through."

Then, to get rid of the envelope clenched between his fingers, he opened it, crumpled it up and threw it under the table.

He was headed towards his room when Maury held him back.

"Don't you want to warm up a little?" he asked, pointing to the bar.

Then he added, with sad irony: "You become such a teetotaller whenever I'm around."

The young man was seized by a profound melancholy. His comrade must have been in such despair over their friendship to want to revive it through such coarse means, which had seemed so repugnant to him not all that long ago. Jean lacked the strength to refuse Claude's pathetic entreaty.

However, their joy at having cheated death gave them some respite from their mutual discomfort. The wine they drank had a more lively flavour than usual. The basic furnishings of the mess hall imparted a feeling of domestic security.

Maury, who'd delayed reading his letter long enough for the light to change, opened the envelope his wife had sent him. Steeped in a primal well-being, Herbillon daydreamed.

Feeling Maury's gaze settle on him, Jean lifted his head and failed to repress a shudder. Maury's features were so filled with fear, mixed with a desire to overcome his incomprehension, that Jean was unable to help himself and asked: "Did you get bad news?"

"Why would you ask me that?" Maury almost shouted.

"You just look so distraught."

Claude jumped off the stool he'd been sitting on and started to walk across the mess hall. Jean was well acquainted with those gangly, robotic walks, whose sole aim was to subdue his excessive emotions. By the time Maury stopped, he'd managed to restore some calm to his features.

"No, you're wrong, it's just that those bullets fried my nerves."

He started reading his letter again, but did so too quickly and too mechanically, the way one sees bad actors in a theatre clumsily pretend to utter a line for the first time when they've in fact spoken it many times before. Suddenly, he said: "Hélène asked me to send news of you."

Herbillon took a long time to swallow the gulp of wine in his mouth.

"Your wife is very kind," he finally muttered.

"You deserve all the credit; Hélène's never usually taken an interest in any of my friends."

"Oh, she's just being polite," Jean said, almost shattering the glass in his hand.

"No, I can assure you that's not the case. Her questions betray a great deal of interest and I'm overjoyed that you're the object of that interest," Claude insisted.

Maury had injected such bitterness into the last words that Jean left without answering him. Claude's dumbfounded eyes wandered around the room.

Absorbed in his daily chores and games, Herbillon failed to reflect on the situation in the manner the occasion called for until later that evening. Its tragedy only struck him fully once he was alone in his room, when the barracks was isolated by the night. He hadn't written to Denise since his return, even thought she'd continued to send him letters expressing her fervent devotion. Having reached the end of her tether, she'd asked Claude for news of him.

Had it been a calculated move on her part to force him to answer her, or simply the end result of her intolerable anxiety? Herbillon shrugged his shoulders. What did it matter whether he knew what had prompted her? He didn't have the right to be indignant, or even angry, especially while his fate was still bound to Maury's, and while Jean still accepted his withering friendship. Jean was such a coward that he hadn't even found the audacity to completely reassure his comrade on that front.

What truly mattered at this given time was the suspicion he'd read in Claude's eyes that morning. Up until that moment, Jean's reticence and coldness, especially his refusal to hug Maury during the medal ceremony, had instilled an atmosphere of treacherous mistrust. Yet it had become overwhelmingly clear that Claude's distrust had solidified, and burrowed its way into his heart.

Jean's silence had been useless. The logic, influence and strength of passions, which still eluded his young mind, was dragging him to the fatal spot which he'd wanted to avoid at all costs. He was seized by the desire to rebel against the inflexibility of a path that Jean still believed he could bend to his will.

Claude would never be able to guess the truth, unless he, Jean Herbillon, allowed him to do so. Maury could have his suspicions and bark up the right tree, but he would never be able to confirm any of them without Jean's confession!

As such, Jean had to overcome the awkwardness caused by his sudden turnaround and recapture Maury's frightened tenderness, resume their long conversations, have Claude confide in him and also pretend to reciprocate. He had to resume his correspondence with Denise to deaden her pain, as well as lay the trap of deception before the truth had a chance to come out. His betrayal would have to be perfect in its baseness.

However, would Jean really be capable of subjecting Claude to such constant, hateful trickery? Claude surely wouldn't let himself be duped, even if he tried. They had become too closely interlinked and, being fellow crewmen, their bond was far too steady for such a blatant lie to pass undetected. That damned connection of theirs certainly wouldn't lead Claude to concrete evidence on its own, but he still wouldn't overlook what was clearly the truth at the heart of the matter.

So what should he do? The young man buried his head in his hands, seeking an elusive compromise between entirely concealing the matter and confessing.

He suddenly experienced the same emotion he'd felt when he *knew* Maury had realized it was him in his cockpit.

"Here I am daydreaming," he murmured. "I have to get some sleep."

He stood up without, however, managing to stifle that distress call. It was as if Claude were dragging Jean towards him with such force that he unconsciously took a step towards the door. Coming round, he began undressing. The mechanical gestures involved in that process swallowed him up again and the dark feelings he'd been fighting against rose up again so powerfully that he no longer doubted what he had to do. Maury's room was calling out for his presence.

He crossed the corridor and quietly opened the latch. Leaning over his desk, Claude had placed two envelopes side by side and was comparing them. Herbillon immediately saw that one of them was the one he'd crumpled and thrown under the table in the mess hall.

Maury welcomed him in, showing no surprise.

"I thought you'd come eventually."

The night had fallen thickly. In the penumbra, the air was perfectly still. They talked very softly, focusing more on their expressions than their words.

"You picked up my envelope," Jean said. "Why?"

"I thought I recognized the handwriting."

"Your wife's?"

Failing to reply, Claude waited. Jean was so tired that he was almost tempted not to put up a fight. Yet faced with Jean's silence, Maury asked him, in a shamefully pleasing manner that distorted his features: "Tell me, it's not true, right?"

Herbillon lied: artfully, sweetly, he showed Claude the childishness and folly of his suspicions. He'd only seen Hélène on a single occasion, and for a very short time at that. How could Maury think that a correspondence could have ensued from such a brief encounter, which had completely revolved around the subject of her husband anyway? And how could he substantiate the hypothesis that his wife would write to another man and then ask her husband about the very same man?

Claude listened to Jean so attentively that it made the blue veins in his forehead bulge. Then he asked Jean:

"So what's caused the distance between us since your return from Paris?"

Jean replied, chanting each word: "There's something in you that pushes people away! Didn't you tell me that yourself?"

When Herbillon left, Claude experienced a moment of peace and relief. After which he murmured: "He was too vicious to be telling the truth."

Nevertheless, the officer cadet's arguments were valid, nay irrefutable. Jean had only gone to visit Hélène the day before his departure. Nothing could have happened over such a short span of time.

Yet, in great distress, Claude realized it could also be a case of argument by *reductio ad absurdum.*

So as not to break up a crew which had proven itself so valiantly after being put to the test, Thélis refused Jean's pleading request that he be assigned to another pilot. The officer cadet also didn't want the captain to mediate the disagreement Thélis thought existed between him and Maury, so the captain added: "You'll have all the time you need to make it up. We're going on holiday at the end of the week."

CHAPTER V

THE GIRLS from the village of Bacoli had dolled themselves up and turned out to witness the arrival of the pilots, and as one after the other jumped out of their cockpits, the pilots were overjoyed to see that colourful crowd, which painted a picture of the tranquil, idle days to come.

The ancient church was festooned with ivy. Nearby, there was a patrician garden around a large mansion whose windows were shut.

The billet he'd drawn at random led Herbillon to a large room upholstered in wallpaper emblazoned with modest flowers. The heavy, polished wooden furniture smelt of fresh wax. Leaving Mathieu to the task of unpacking his trunk, the officer cadet went to seek out Thélis so he could receive his orders.

"You're on vacation," Thélis told the assembled officers. "I'm going to take advantage of the situation and go on leave myself. Maury will be in charge during my absence. Have fun and don't make too much of a racket."

The soldiers took the girls out to the big park where, thanks to the July heat, the leaves were motionless and spread out to the light. The planes were kept locked inside the hangars and, in order to seduce difficult hearts, only the very young pilots would occasionally take them out to perform acrobatics that could easily have landed them with broken necks.

Herbillon quickly discovered that Bacoli didn't really cater to his tastes. Whenever he dragged his boots over the swaying grass that slept under the trees and tried to start up an affair with one of the village's unsavoury beauties, he would find himself oppressed by a hideous boredom. He tried to read, but he quickly realized that he couldn't persevere with any book that wasn't mindless, and so he began longing for the squadron's cursory routine, where the days went by quickly and monotonously.

Maury lived in the house where the offices were situated. He signed documents, ensured the soldiers' meals were served on time and meandered through the patrician gardens' solitary paths. The dreams, thoughts and doubts that absorbed him rendered him immune to the passing of time. However, having examined every aspect of his new relationship with Jean, he had reached a conclusion that soothed his worries: the officer cadet had fallen prey to his wife's charms and, uncompromising to the extreme, had decided that this new fondness was incompatible with the demands of their friendship.

Maury also allowed for the fact his wife would have fallen for his friend's charms too. Yet their meeting hadn't led to any complications or consequences, and thus this problem was bound to be transitory. Maury gradually reassured himself and began discovering his wife's letters were marked by a greater tenderness and betrayed deeper thoughts and emotions.

The vacation imposed on their squadron made Maury and Herbillon less sensitive to each others' presence, allowing them to cool down. A kind of truce was established between them.

Whenever Herbillon, shuffling along, oppressed by his idleness, came across Maury's silhouette, he would instantly feel the need to talk to him. Yet they would only exchange a few words, which were always vague and neutral. How far their hour-long conversations had receded into the past.

After their brief meetings, Herbillon would find his boredom even more intolerable, especially since he'd imagined this leisure time would have been filled with pleasures and merry-making.

Thus, he was truly pleased when Pilot Officer Narbonne came to suggest an idea for a regular series of poker games.

This officer had taken up residence in a low-ceilinged room in the village's only inn, which was cluttered with framed photographs, fake flowers and pious icons. That evening, Herbillon met up with Charensole, Michel, Virense and Doc in that room. Amidst laughter, they told him how Marbot, having been approached about the game, had refused with a savage vehemence. On the table was a bottle of cognac, a box of cigars and several decks of cards. The smoke had already changed the light emanating from the lamps. Herbillon breathed it in with sheer delight.

He'd thus escaped the dreariness of his nights, and had been rescued from the village's little streets, which he'd acquainted himself with in the space of just a couple of nights, to the point where the mere sight of them filled him with nausea. He'd been saved from the lonely alcohol consumed with his elbows propped atop a sticky table. This escape pleased him to such an extent that he didn't even bother to ask how much the chips that had been placed in front of him were worth. Narbonne, who was wealthy, showed the same reckless indifference. Their comrades took advantage of this. They only rose from their seats once the dawn had washed the night's inky stains from the windows, when Jean eventually realized he'd lost his entire pay. Yet since his parents sent him twice that sum every month, he didn't regret it.

He was more careful the following evening, but his impetuous nature meant he was not on a level playing field with his comrades, for whom the game was nothing but a fleeting amusement. Jean, on the other hand, loved risk for risk's sake, and was simply incapable of playing a hand without betting more than he could reasonably afford. He was gripped by the giddiness of the fast pace of assembling a combination of cards.

Knowing this, he usually abstained from playing, but he always succumbed the moment he actually sat down at the table.

The sound of drunken refrains and the echo of lighthearted quarrels from the room below rose through the floorboards. Being better nourished, blood flowed more abundantly through their veins. The success of a risky hand filled Jean with enormous pride and a victorious feeling that made all his other triumphs pale in comparison. A loud bell rang in his ear and a special, artificial sort of bliss ran through his entire body, like a narcotic.

From that moment on, he became a prisoner of the game. His entire life, an empty canvas, oscillated around the axis formed by the hours he spent at Narbonne's place. He would get up very late, while the afternoons would slide past him in a monochrome haze, his eyes bloodshot from the previous all-nighter. His entire body was imbued with exhaustion, distracting him from his boredom. As the twilight gave way to darkness, his appetite for gambling would wake him up and, re-energized by an adulterated, yet powerful joy, he would climb the steps to the room where the cards awaited him. So long as he sat at that magic table, he was bewitched by a spell.

Nevertheless, he kept losing and soon enough ran out of money. Narbonne fronted him a loan, coupled with some advice to take care. Jean listened to him distractedly but, despite how difficult it proved for him to do so, he also asked his father for more money.

He lost all of it over the course of three games and had to turn to his comrade yet again. On that evening, before the game started, Doc told Narbonne: "Mercier asked me if he could join us."

Narbonne hesitated. Wouldn't the presence of Major Mercier, the division commander, oblige them to exercise some restraint given the latter's stripes and seniority? Furthermore, Mercier was known throughout the entire air force as a sharp-witted, dangerous card player and, although he never placed a low bet, he always won. His presence could quickly disturb the balance of a game where, although one could lose a lot of money, excessive bets were deliberately avoided.

"Does he have his heart set on it?" Narbonne asked.

"Quite," Doc replied.

The following day, Major Mercier sat at their table. He was a square-shouldered, square-jawed man with a square forehead. His face looked like a wooden mask with very bright eyes which betrayed a gloomy, ill-restrained rage, as well as an insatiable desire for risk. Even though his duties and rank forbade him from flying, he often took a fighter plane out on his own and went out on patrols. Everyone admired his courage, but nobody loved him.

Nevertheless, the major quickly knew how to dispel the unease his appearance had caused and appeared to gladly take part in a game that was too meek and modest for his own taste. After an hour, seeing that Narbonne and Herbillon kept losing, as usual, he exclaimed: "You're playing really badly. We're going to skin you alive!"

"We've had a lot of practice when it comes to losing, Major," Narbonne replied.

"No, I must insist, it shames me to take so much of your money. Let's play Shimmy instead, at least you might stand a chance with that."

"It's a little dangerous," Doc said. "We'll get carried away."

"Come on, let's start small. One louis a hand."

The officers yielded. Narbonne began. He lost right away. The game went on, hand after hand, with varying degrees of success, while everyone noticed that Mercier limited himself to watching the game without taking part.

When it was his turn to the banker dealer, he casually pulled out a 100 franc note and said: "I'm afraid I don't have any change, gentlemen, but don't feel obliged to cover my bet."

As there were a few of them playing, it worked out easily. Mercier won. He banked 200 francs. Then he won again.

"Twenty louis, *banco*," he said leisurely.

A few hands placed some small, partial bets. In order to pleasure the major, Narbonne proclaimed: "I'll take the bet."

Mercier still played the better hand.

He looked at the sum, which had since doubled, and pondered.

"I'll deal again," Mercier said.

"I'll still take the bet," Narbonne said.

He lost. The major picked up the banknotes, pushed the cards away and jokingly asked: "So who's going to be the banker now?"

Narbonne thought he detected a challenge in the major's sentence: was Mercier looking for another match, or was this simply that unavoidable time of night when one became oblivious to the meaning of money? He couldn't tell, but his astonished comrades heard him exclaim: "I will, Major."

He laid out sixteen 100-franc notes.

"I never play the first hand against the bank, it's up to you, gentlemen!" Mercier said.

Everyone placed small, partial bets. Once the cards were dealt, Narbonne played his hand—he had a nine.

"Hey, good for you!" Mercier exclaimed.

The officers saw the same cruel, voracious sparkle in Mercier's eyes that made them gleam whenever he flew off in his fighter plane.

"*Banco*," he said.

He looked at his cards and declared: "I'll stand pat."

Narbonne had a three.

"I think I've struck a bad deal," he said, taking another card. It was a five.

"Good draw," the major said. "It cost me 100 louis, are you going to stop?"

"No, I'll keep going."

"Very well then, *banco*!"

Narbonne drew a nine again. Mercier handed over 4,000 francs.

A great silence filled the room, because everyone knew that the major lived entirely off his army pay. Yet his square face didn't twitch in the slightest and his voice was very calm when he said: "This hand passed seven times, that's unusual."

Embarrassed, Narbonne rapped his fingers on the table. He didn't want to quit the game after having won so much but, on the other hand, how could he possibly continue? His eyes met the major's and, despite their hardness, he thought he could see a kind of entreaty in them, which made him feel bad. He made the following suggestion: "Would you like to play again, Major?"

"Gladly!"

All eyes were fixed on them. Eight thousand francs were at stake, and the morbid attraction of instant gain, the uncertainty of luck and the size of the sum being played for seemed to rise from the table like unhealthy fumes.

"I'd like a card," Mercier said.

But on seeing the King that Narbonne dealt him, his jaws clenched.

Narbonne had pulled a six, and thus won the game when, to everyone's surprise, he drew another card.

"He must be crazy," Herbillon thought, "or maybe he just wants to lose."

Narbonne drew a three. He was doing even better.

"I owe you 8,000 francs, old chap," Mercier said, pretending to get up.

"No, Major, I couldn't possibly leave you like this. Would you like to play another game to redeem your debt?"

"Double or nothing!" Mercier exclaimed, his voice echoing far too loudly in that little room.

Doc whispered in Herbillon's ear: "He could probably pay off the 8,000, just about, but *16,000*? Never!"

"But he's bound to win, you see—it's just a matter of mathematics."

This time, Mercier's fingers trembled slightly as they gripped the cards. He drew an eight. Narbonne drew a nine.

The discomfort in the room was such that the officers hung their heads to avoid seeing the major's face. Without hesitating, Mercier said:

"*Banco*. Thirty-two thousand francs."

Even if he'd wanted to, Narbonne couldn't have shied away from the challenge, and he won again.

Mercier persisted in playing double of nothing for another three times and lost on each occasion. He now owed Narbonne half a million. Everyone thought he seemed as though he was about to sink into an abyss.

That Narbonne continued to accept his bets was merely the result of a subordinate being charitable to his commanding officer.

No one could tell who was more tormented by the situation: the major, who was getting thrashed, which was unusual for him, or Narbonne, who would have gladly cheated just in order to lose if he could be certain no one would catch him in the act.

Nevertheless, the game had to go on.

Mercier had even stopped saying "*Banco*!", and Narbonne didn't even bring the issue up. He merely continued dealing the cards, looking at them, drawing others when he didn't even need them, and yet still continued to win.

Narbonne kept winning, damned by a lucky streak, as the sequence of cards he drew inevitably gave him the upper hand. It defied all calculations, probabilities and likelihood, and it seemed set to persist throughout the whole night.

After having won eighteen times, Narbonne finally lost.

Mercier stood up and left without a word, not deigning to touch the money on the table, which he'd rightfully won.

Nobody said a single word or made a single gesture to try to detain him.

That very morning, when the major went out in his plane to try out a new engine, he was killed on the spot. Afraid to vent their thoughts, the officers who'd assembled in the mess hall said: "Another loss of momentum."

When the group met again that night at Narbonne's, their voices were subdued. They rarely spoke, but they played cards furiously. Far from serving as a warning,

Mercier's adventure had piqued their passions. The sums that had been gambled away the previous night had now cast a spell on them. Their grasp on the value of money was completely skewed. Their hardened faces and the curtness of their speech betrayed the primitive instinct to win that was making them forsake the many ties that bound those men in friendship. One would have said that Death was keeping its pale eyes fixed on them. Narbonne, whose fortune had imparted him with a relative indifference to money, felt scared whenever he looked his comrades in the eye.

Far more susceptible to the dead major's influence than anyone else in that group, and believing that the cards in his hands held the very essence of his life, Herbillon's foolish audacity was unmatched by any of the others.

When he got back to his room, where the flowers on the wallpaper already emerged out of the shadows, Jean threw himself on the bed without even removing his boots, wanting to fall asleep right away so he could forget everything. He had lost 8,000 francs' worth of IOUs. Yet sleep wouldn't come to him.

The images of Bloody Hearts, Flat Diamonds, Mottled Clubs and Spades with their funerary spikes, the impassive, mysterious faces of Kings, Queens and Jacks, flashed past him under his feverish eyelids, under his aching forehead, like a bedevilled crowd, a procession of the damned.

Giving up the fight against that devilish influence, the young man headed towards the open window that gave onto the summer dawn. The scent of peppermint carnations wafted up like a wave from the garden below. A thin, pinkish strip on the horizon gently gnawed away at the sky's darkness. Witnessing the breaking of a pure, pristine morning, Jean felt miserable and soiled.

Mercier's death had alerted the entire squadron to the existence of Narbonne's card-playing sessions, and Claude had no difficulty in figuring out the root cause behind the crazed look on Herbillon's face. The remaining tenderness he still felt for that young man was now compounded by a feeling of responsibility towards him. After all, hadn't the captain entrusted him with his comrades' well-being?

He took hold of the officer cadet's arm and this gesture filled Jean with gratitude. How badly he needed some help and support on that day! The image of Denise was completely effaced by the calamity he now found himself in.

They walked in silence all the way to the vast gardens, where the light and the heat flowed in attenuated waves.

"Did you lose a great deal of money?" Maury gently asked him.

"Far too much!"

"Nothing to despair over… you're young and idle…"

Then he added, thus removing any hint of reproach: "…and you feel you should be allowed to do whatever you want because our most likely fate that destiny has in store for us is death."

Claude's words worked like a soothing balm on Herbillon's suffering. They offered excuses at a time when Jean felt he could no longer forgive himself, having already done so on too many occasions. Jean bitterly reflected how it had been exactly one of those excuses that had led him into the arms of the wife who belonged to the man who was consoling him.

Enfeebled by his anxiety and sleep deprivation, he murmured: "Oh! If things hadn't changed between the two of us, I wouldn't have taken things that far…"

An emotion Jean was too well acquainted with lit up Maury's eyes.

"Jean," he said, "nothing on this earth ever dies completely. For the time being, promise me you won't go to Narbonne's any more."

He'd injected such affection into his voice that the young man momentarily thought their friendship appeared ready to be made new.

"At least let me try to recoup my losses, then I'll stop, I swear."

"Give it up, you'll be better off that way."

"I can't. I lost too much."

"How much?"

"Eight thousand," Jean whispered.

"Listen," Claude firmly told him, "I'll loan you the money. You can pay me back in instalments."

Claude instantly turned pale. Jean had pushed him away with a brutal, lifeless gesture. The abhorrence Maury felt at the young man's refusal reawakened in him a horror that he thought he'd laid to rest for good, albeit in a harsher and more definite form.

CHAPTER VI

A LARGE SIGN was displayed in the front window of the Café de la Poste, which was situated on the main square. In huge, clumsily scrawled letters, it announced that the café was under new management and was now run by "*Mademoiselle Paméla, formerly of the Saint-Martin Casino*".

The girl was tall, common and rather beautiful: buxom, with thick, coppery locks and meaty lips. She kept tirelessly singing lazy love songs, risqué rhymes, drank a lot and successfully encouraged others to do so too.

This was where Marbot took Herbillon the following evening.

Standing on the cabaret's threshold, the officer cadet thought everything about it—the smoke-filled room, the clamour, the brutally animated figures—was simply repulsive.

"What's the matter?"

"Don't you see? There's nowhere to sit."

"Nowhere to sit!" Marbot exclaimed. "I'd be surprised if there wasn't any room for veterans of the 39. Landlady!"

Marbot's powerful voice overcame the noise and attracted Paméla's attention just as she was getting ready to sing. She slowly furrowed her thick eyebrows, or rather her monobrow. Her success had sharpened her impatience and authoritativeness. She didn't let men of Marbot's type boss her around in the slightest.

An insult was about to slip out of her lips when she laid eyes on Herbillon. He was so handsome and sad—the kind of carnal sadness women always fall for—that Paméla hesitated, then left the rickety platform that served as her stage.

"You shouldn't outstay your welcome when all you drink is red wine," she told two artillery farriers. "I need you to give up your table!"

"But we want to listen to you sing," one of them protested.

"You can hear me just as well standing up."

They obeyed the sound of her voice, as well as her thick, red lips.

"Over here, my little pilot!" she exclaimed.

"You see?" Marbot told him, looking smug. "I only have to snap my fingers to make it so…"

A waitress approached them. They ordered hard liquor.

Paméla went back to her stage.

She sang with a sharp, convincing tone and a raspy solemnity that gave her otherwise common voice and coarse gestures a greater authority. The room obediently accepted her sensual and tender invitations. Through the slow undulations of thick smoke, one could see her primal, serene face emerge distorted, swollen and exaggerated, as though it were a mask.

Perhaps the only one in the room to do so, Herbillon avoided looking at Paméla. The primal nature of the spectacle inspired an aversion in him that bordered on hatred. Far too young still to discern that his loathing was caused by the fact he saw himself reflected in that girl, Jean felt an intense annoyance swell within him, an unsavoury hatred that wasn't directed at anything or anyone.

He tried to assuage it by drinking, but his unease wasn't the sort that could be quelled by alcohol; in fact, thanks to his moody impatience, drinking was only bound to exacerbate it.

When Paméla finished, the crowd rose in a chorus: "Encore!"

"Sing us another!"

"Don't be lazy!"

She regally shook her coppery locks and replied: "I'm singing myself to death here and you want more! My throat's on fire!"

She went to sit with a police officer with swarthy skin and a vain moustache, who waited for her with a bottle of champagne in front of him as though he owned the place. While letting the police officer touch her fleshy shoulders, Paméla kept searching for Herbillon's gaze.

"What a glorious filly!" Marbot exclaimed. "I'd ride her bareback!"

"No accounting for taste!" Jean retorted, in an almost wounding manner.

His companion observed: "You weren't always this difficult…"

"You don't say!"

Placing his big fists on the table, Marbot told him: "In any case, I'm warning you that I'm going to invite her over for a drink, whether you like it or not."

"You can do so on your own."

"As you like. I'm not going to force you."

The only desire Herbillon felt within him—that of leaving—was disappointed by those words. They made him realize that the only things waiting for him outside were the night, the silence and his own thoughts.

"I don't want to miss out on the show," he said sarcastically, "but I'll watch from a distance..."

A table freed up on the other side of the room and Jean thus parted with Marbot, who muttered: "You're really out of it today, cadet..."

This little argument hadn't eluded the attentions of Paméla, who kept an unfailing watch over her realm.

"I have to go over there," she told the police officer, "those new customers don't look that happy to me."

She freed herself from the officer's arm, which was clasped around her waist, and approached Marbot.

"Did you have a fight with your friend?" she asked him.

Marbot's eyes stealthily drifted towards Herbillon who, with his head hung low, no longer heard or saw anything, except the already drained glass in front of him, and was completely absorbed in his sad reverie.

"There are never any serious disputes between the two of us, my beauty!" Marbot cheerfully replied. "I don't blame him. The boy's been completely different ever since he came back from his leave. He must be heartbroken."

A deep sense of compassion weakened Paméla's muscles, the same kind of feeling she experienced whenever she walked through the streets of a lower-class neighbourhood and heard a plaintive love song.

"Heartbroken..." she said. "Such a handsome boy..."

"That's exactly the kind of boy these things happen to, of course! It's because they take themselves too seriously! Will you drink with me?"

"I won't turn you down if you offer me one some other time, but not tonight, my policeman is jealous."

"Well, I'm on his turf here... I understand..."

Marbot hung his head and, in a mutter, added: "Policemen... they're worse than Fokkers."

Paméla took a few steps back towards her table, hesitated, then turned towards Herbillon. She couldn't resist the allure of that smooth forehead, which the officer cadet held tightly in his hands. Paméla couldn't overcome her desire.

The officer cadet suddenly heard a soft, shy voice that was very close to him say: "Aren't you feeling well? Perhaps you've drunk too much?"

He shuddered, looked at the singer for a moment uncomprehendingly and then brutally replied: "Too much? You mean not enough, right? But there's nothing strong to drink here. Tell them to bring me a real man's drink."

The warm, generous body leaning over Herbillon was overcome with great pity.

"You're going to hurt yourself…"

"So this is a cabaret only fit for little girls then?"

The singer called a waitress over.

"Marthe, bring over some of *my* grappa," she ordered.

Slipping her a sly gesture, she quickly added in a whisper: "The cheap one."

The officer cadet had once again stopped paying attention to anything going on around him. However, the singer couldn't bring herself to leave him on his own. She felt the need to talk to him, but didn't know what to say. Finally, she asked him: "So, you're a pilot?"

A twitch made Jean's jaws clench.

"You can see that I am," he replied.

"Still so young and you already have a medal on your chest?"

"That wasn't my fault!"

Instead of wounding Paméla or chasing her away, Jean merely managed to pull on her heart strings even more. That lordly tone in a teenage shell… that repressed anger… that raw, beautiful sorrow… moved to pity, the girl had fallen for him and was ready to be in love.

"Can I sit with you for a little while?" she pleaded.

"Why?"

She humbly replied: "I'd like to offer you something."

"Oh no, I'll make you as miserable as I am."

"If you insist."

"Oh, you know…"

Herbillon didn't have the time to finish his thought. The police officer yelled: "Paméla!"

Without bothering to reply to him, and as though she hadn't heard him, Paméla calmly applied some thick rouge to her lips.

"Paméla!" the officer repeated, raising his voice. "Do I really need to run after you?"

A kind of morbid delight electrified Herbillon's nerves. The target-less rage that had been building up in him ever since he'd set foot inside that cabaret finally found the right pretext to burst. It was an outburst that needed to happen, an essential act of catharsis.

"Why don't you relax, you little draft-dodger?" he said, half getting up from his table. "Paméla is sitting at my table and she can stay here as long as she likes!"

"Oh, my little one," Paméla gratefully and cheerfully murmured, "you want to stand up for me..."

Herbillon pushed past the naked shoulder pressing against him and advanced towards his adversary.

Amidst the silence the room had plunged into, the police officer mumbled: "Wannabe... brat... greenhorn..."

His invectives were shattered by the painful cry he voiced.

Herbillon had grabbed hold of his moustache and was pulling on it almost to the point of ripping it off. The policeman raised his hand. The officers present in the room left their table to go break up the brawl. There was no need for them to do so. Marbot had already separated the men. Shaking the policeman with all his formidable might, he growled: "Get out of here, Fokker. The little one here is my friend. Get out of here, it's for the best!"

Everyone in the room was hostile to the policeman's presence. He was forced to withdraw.

Despite Paméla's protests, Herbillon and Marbot left right after him.

*

Herbillon woke up the next morning with a feeling of peace he hadn't experienced in a long time.

"Rest, finally some real rest..." he murmured, leaping out of bed.

Outside, the sun shone on the slate roofs. Specks of dust that seemed to have been born from those rays of light danced around. Herbillon had his one-eyed orderly help him shower in the courtyard, then rapidly dressed himself.

"My lieutenant finally looks healthy this morning," the old soldier said.

"It's all because I behaved badly last night, Mathieu."

"Get it out of your system while you're still young, Lieutenant!"

Herbillon was out on the street, whistling the squadron's tune, when a sentry approached him and blocked his path.

"Lieutenant Maury has asked for you," he told him, out of breath. "Urgent business."

It wasn't a long walk to the office where Maury was waiting for him, but Herbillon found it tougher than a forced march. He knew why Maury had sent for him and he wasn't worried about it at all. What really oppressed him, which deprived him of the zest for life which he had for a few moments reacquired in a wonderfully vigorous manner, was the necessity to attend the meeting to which he was headed.

He interpreted it as a fatal sign, a seal that would be impossible to break. The noose that bound them together, which they thought they'd slipped out of, was now mercilessly tightening around their necks, binding their destinies together. Herbillon felt all this with a concealed terror when he glimpsed into Maury's eyes, which no longer betrayed suspicion as they once did, but rather a kindness and concern that filled Jean with shame, regret and a fondness that was more painful to bear than his unforgivable mistakes.

"Can I be of assistance?" he asked, in as offhand a manner as he could manage, trying to sound as official as possible.

Claude didn't allow himself to be fooled by Jean's affectations. He was the squadron's commander for the time being and, just like Thélis before him, he wanted to run it like a big brother.

"Herbillon," he sweetly began, "why didn't you come talk to me about that silly business?"

"What silly business?"

"Come on, you know what I mean. Your quarrel with that policeman. I have his complaint right here; would you like to read it?"

"I have no interest in it. Do whatever you think is best."

A sad crease which Herbillon was far too well acquainted with formed around the corners of Maury's lips. Claude smiled and continued: "I'll take care of the matter, naturally… but do me a favour and make sure it doesn't happen again. I know you won't want to put me in such a difficult situation again in Thélis's absence. Getting completely drunk like that is so unlike you, after all."

"I wasn't drunk," Herbillon said.

Jean was at the end of his tether. Claude's affectionate tone, the words he was using, his desire to protect him, to help him, he just couldn't face it any more. Accepting his help… reaching the nadir of humiliation, of deceit…

"You don't really expect me to believe this was all over some girl?" Claude exclaimed.

Herbillon was frightened by Claude's overly penetrating gaze. He needed to bring that meeting to an end as soon as possible.

"At least I wasn't accountable to you back up north," he said. "If you have to punish me, then go ahead, I won't beg you to spare me. But I'm free to do what I like when I'm off-duty."

When Herbillon left, Maury lingered pensively for a moment.

Then, for the hundredth time that day, he reread his wife's letter. She was coming to join him. The train would drop her off at the station in an hour's time. It would be a long wait!

CHAPTER VII

THE PLATFORMS were almost empty. There were a few police officers and a sergeant wearing a helmet with a chin strap who led a unit of soldiers, who were busy inspecting the papers of the soldiers on leave. As soon as the train began to slow down, the young woman had no trouble recognizing her husband's tall, frail frame. Her feelings towards him hadn't changed, and were the usual mix of friendship, security and indifference.

Yet how her blood grew hot when her desire led her to believe, against all likelihood, that the young staff officer in the distance was her Herbillon!

"I must really be losing my mind," she said to herself once she realized her mistake. "Claude must have come on his own."

Maury had also recognized Hélène from afar. By the time her head appeared out of the carriage door, and she bent that long, supple neck which he so dearly loved, nothing remained of his former doubts and anxiety.

Hélène had come to him, to be with him, and had set off after barely having received the news that he was on vacation. She had come to him with her bright, lively eyes, her youthful movements and her secret seriousness.

At that moment, Maury was so happy that he childishly thought his temporary command of the squadron was a mark of great prestige. He wanted to jump onto the still-moving train and leap from footboard to footboard to reach the woman who so thrilled him with delight. But she still intimidated him, just like she'd always done.

It was precisely when he was in Hélène's presence that Claude felt most hindered by his awkwardness, his body's lack of gracefulness and his inability to convey his emotions.

Thus, Maury waited until the train had come to a complete stop and, by the time he advanced towards Hélène, nothing of his earlier feelings were left except a welcoming expression that was very calm and considerate. She thought he was examining her, as though his cool, lucid affection was judging her. She felt the need to apologize: "I just couldn't stand it any more, Claude," she told him. "I promise I won't bother you while you're among your comrades."

He clasped her against his bony body with a passion that was so timid it was almost impossible to perceive and, even though his heart was overflowing with happiness and gratitude, he quietly replied: "You did the right thing, darling. My comrades don't impinge much on my life."

She took his arm. They left the station without exchanging any more words. As they were being driven away, Maury could no longer entirely conceal the intensity of his happiness: "Hélène, Hélène…" he murmured. "I've thought so much about you! You've rescued me from my solitude, my demons…"

She barely heard him. Right up to the last moment when they'd left the station, her eyes had kept scanning her surroundings for Herbillon. Even though she constantly felt at fault in Maury's presence, she didn't feel guilty about the one thing he could have actually reproached her for.

"You're so sweet," she replied, absent-mindedly.

The squadron's quartermaster had found a nice big room and a kitchen to set up the officers' mess, which was situated in a genteel mansion on the outskirts of town.

Herbillon headed over there at lunchtime. Thanks to the long brisk walk, he'd managed to dispel the unease that his meeting with Maury had caused him. He reaped the blessings of all that sun, the beautiful flower-studded fields, the sweetly scorching air and the dust raised by his boots as he walked down the path.

The way his comrades welcomed him imparted to him a boyish sense of pleasure. They were proud of how he'd conducted himself at Paméla's. He had defended the squadron's honour. Not satisfied with having conquered the heart of the most sought-after woman in Bacoli, he'd also given a police officer a rightly deserved hiding!

"We'll never go out in a finer blaze of glory," Narbonne solemnly said. "Let me buy you a tall glass!"

Everyone drank to Herbillon's adventure, and Jean himself was close to thinking he'd behaved admirably.

Marbot suddenly entered and, while still standing on the threshold, shouted to the orderlies: "Add another setting, next to Lieutenant Maury."

Then, turning to the officers, he added: "Bide your tongues, no cursing, or he'll have you cooked alive!"

"Who's going to eat with us?" Doc asked. "A colonel, a general?"

"Even better—a woman! Maury's wife."

Herbillon slowly backed away, his hands limp and moist, while Marbot carried on: "Maury called me so I could apologize to you. Since his wife has just arrived, he didn't want to bother us by eating here, but I protested, nay demanded he lunch with us, and in the end he agreed. Did I do the right thing?"

"It wouldn't have been decent of you not to," Doc said.

"And besides, she might be pretty! Have you seen her?" Narbonne asked.

"Unfortunately not," Marbot said. "She was busy unpacking in the room above Maury's office, but Herbillon met her when he was on leave in Paris."

"Oh!... Only very briefly," Jean said, with some effort.

"Well, how was she?"

"Younger than him."

"And?"

"She's... not bad at all... You'll see for yourselves."

The officers instinctively straightened their jackets and tightened their belts.

"If I'd known she was coming I would have worn my new boots," Narbonne exclaimed. "I want to go change right away."

"You won't have the time," Marbot said. "She'll be here any minute."

Herbillon was overcome with panic. He felt he couldn't deal with both Maury and Denise at the same time—and in front of the whole squadron to boot! Denise, who of course was in reality called Hélène. His mistress—who was actually Claude's wife.

He'd never really been able to merge the two in his mind, and bind those different roles into a single person. He thought he could easily lose his mind if he saw Denise standing next to Maury, and perhaps start screaming, pleading and raving…

A little door led out into the courtyard. He slipped towards it and vanished.

A few minutes later, Maury introduced his wife to all the officers. She listened to their names—Marbot, Doc—as though she was in the midst of a confused dream. The only face she wanted to see, as though driven by some maddening thirst, was nowhere to be found.

"Herbillon's still missing," Maury finally said. "You remember him, don't you, Hélène, the young cadet I sent over to meet you?"

She nodded, incapable of uttering a word. If Herbillon had been there, everything would have seemed easier, more straightforward. Without him, she felt empty, forsaken, indifferent to everything.

The following sentences reawakened her interest.

"The cad… but he was here with us just a moment ago!" Narbonne exclaimed. "There's his half-empty glass of port right there."

"He just ran away!" Doc exclaimed.

Lowering his voice, Marbot added: "He was afraid we'd hold him back and he wanted to go see Paméla."

Doc smiled, nodded, and went from officer to officer to slip them the news.

"Why don't we sit?" Maury suggested.

The brawl between Herbillon and the policeman was the main topic of conversation. Marbot related it down to the smallest detail.

"Did he really pull the Fokker's moustache?" Narbonne asked, over the moon. "His enormous moustache. Isn't that scandalous, Madame?"

"I can't help but agree," Hélène Maury said, forcing a smile.

The meal went on in the usual noisy, cheerful manner for everyone there, all except for the young woman—whom the officers thought they could amuse with tales of their games, libations or death—and for Claude, who could feel his wife's unease and yet felt powerless to do anything about it.

"If only Thélis had been here," Claude sadly thought to himself.

While his comrades praised and envied his amorous exploits, Herbillon had sought refuge in his room, upholstered in that time-weathered wallpaper, lying motionless on top of his bed, without having even bothered to remove the duvet. His body was half-wrapped in a soft, thick, burning material, while his thoughts whirled around in his head in an infernal circle. He was overwhelmed, haunted, wiped out.

Yet just as he was finding it impossible to move his limbs, even by a single inch, he was also unable to free himself from the web of images in his mind and he found himself confined by the two names that kept haunting him.

Hélène… Denise…

Denise… Hélène…

The same syllables repeatedly hammered away at his brain, and the same frighteningly familiar, frighteningly beloved features kept constantly disappearing and reforming in front of his eyes. It was his whole universe.

He only snapped out of it when Mathieu pushed open the door to his room, and without waiting to be invited in, Denise appeared on the threshold.

At that moment, Herbillon experienced a quasi-miraculous relief. Faced with this woman standing before him in the flesh, whose expressions and sensual density he recognized, the other vague, impossible image of her in his mind, which had paralysed him with a hypnotic kind of terror, completely disappeared. However, as soon as Jean had leaped out of bed and dismissed the orderly with a wave of his hand, he realized what that woman's presence in his room would mean vis-à-vis his relationship to Maury and the squadron, with his comrades walking past the house, while the office where Claude performed his duties as acting commander lay just across the street, surrounded as he was on all sides by the rules of discipline, the army and, ultimately, war.

Without kissing her or coming close to her, Jean asked her in a low voice: "Why did you come here?"

Denise was so completely thrown by that tone in his voice, and by that reproach and fear, that she leaned her back against the door. Separated from her lover by the vastness of that room, she first tried to reassure him.

"Nobody saw me come in here, I swear, Jean," she said. "And I only figured out where you lived by chance; I didn't ask any of your comrades. I couldn't resist… I couldn't wait any longer."

"Why did you come to Bacoli?" the cadet persisted with fierce obstinacy.

The young woman lingered in silence for a moment. However, despite staring at her pointedly, Herbillon didn't notice that her face was hardening. He continued to think out loud.

"I had hoped," he exclaimed, "to find a little respite here… to find myself again… to gain some clarity… that it might be easier away from my duties and all those hours spent flying. Claude had also started to calm down."

Denise's lips barely opened as she replied: "Do you think I came all this way to see *him*? I came here because I had to! You were driving me crazy with your silence. Not a word ever since you left Paris! And thanks to Claude, I knew you were still alive. I had to see you, to know what you wanted, what your thoughts were and if you still had any feelings for me."

Denise walked up to Jean, who looked—his face being so immobile and impassive—as though he hadn't heard her at all.

Truth be told, he hadn't understood any of Denise's words. Yet despite the fact that their meaning had eluded him, he had felt the straightforwardness of her tone, which had come at him rapidly, brutally hammering home its message. What Jean truly perceived were the emotions that went beyond the words: her willpower, which answered to nothing except her passion, an obstinate insatiable desire, which was so honest it was almost barbaric. He felt lost.

Up until that moment, and throughout the time this drama had unfolded, he'd believed he and Maury were the only participants. He'd always thought of Denise as a passive bystander, a catastrophic mistake, an irresponsible object of desire. But now there she was: strong, decisive and forceful, with nothing standing in the way of her passion.

She was taking charge of the situation with a blind, terrible force that was both possessive and destructive. The game was no longer limited to the two officers. A woman had now suddenly intruded upon it to settle it in her own manner and, despite his inexperience, Herbillon confusedly understood that she held a trump card in her hands: a ruthless, primal deity and that was calling out the name of love.

Denise took hold of Jean's face and caressed it, bewitched it, and with wet, shining eyes, she pleaded in a doleful, earnest way: "Tell me I still mean something to you Jean… tell me that you still love me a little."

"Do I even know any more?… Do you think I can still make sense of anything? I no longer know if I hate you, if I hate Maury. Oh, but I do know that I hate myself!"

His face and voice betrayed such agony that Denise forgot her own suffering and inexorable passion for a moment. Sweetly, she asked him: "Why torture yourself like this? You had accepted the situation fully… it was so simple. Do you remember our last night together? When you'd discovered the whole truth?"

"For heaven's sake, shut up!" Jean groaned. "What we did that night is exactly what I find so unforgivable about all this… before that, it was just a horrible coincidence, but after it… Oh, after it!… It's enough to make one lose his mind! Flying together, fighting together, drinking together, being awarded a medal together! How could I possibly write to you? And about what? You've just seen the others eating and laughing shoulder to shoulder—how they are now is what I never will be again: proud and with a clean conscience, safe in the thought I haven't betrayed my crew! *Now* do you understand?"

"That I don't mean anything to you any more, yes I understand that!" Denise retorted, instantly sliding back into her rage, abiding only by her own laws. "Do you need any reasons when you're really in love? None of these things matter to me: Claude, my reputation, social conventions, I would wreck them all for a single, loving word! *The crew*, yes, that's all very nice and noble… but isn't my love for you also nice and noble? If you really cared about Claude so much, then why did you come back to me that evening? Oh, let me speak… Yes, that night, when we were closer than we've ever been."

Herbillon no longer had any strength or resolve. Deaf and stubborn as she was, Denise would simply contradict everything he said and see his greatest defeat as her greatest victory.

Since he'd already given in to her once, she now assumed he would always give in to her. He couldn't stand to be reminded of that shameful, delirious night. He miserably decided to use her own weapon against her. "If you really love me, then shut up, please shut up…"

"*If* I love you?" she shouted, having been wounded exactly where Herbillon had aimed. "Look at my eyes, touch my shoulders!"

"I forbid you," he ordered her. "I forbid you to come any closer. I've thought about you too much, thought about your body..."

By talking about his desire, Herbillon had triggered a fatal chain reaction and revived her passion. His eyes clouded over, while Denise's beamed with a lustrous joy. She finally felt he was hers once again.

Their faces drew closer together. Marbot's voice boomed behind the door.

"Open up, cadet!" the big lieutenant yelled.

Herbillon pushed her away so suddenly, in order to put some distance between them, that Denise staggered.

"I have to show my face, if only for a minute," the cadet whispered, "otherwise he might get suspicious... Find somewhere to hide in here."

Denise slipped into a closet where Herbillon had set up a washbasin.

"I thought you'd gone to see Paméla, but she said she hadn't seen you. So I was worried you might be sick. Are you all right?"

"I am sick, old chap, I am."

"Why did you bunk off lunch like that?"

"Last night's booze hadn't quite worn off."

Marbot sat on the bed and lit a cigarette.

"About last night… there won't be any follow-up. Maury gave me his word. He's a decent guy, that Maury. We really misjudged him at the beginning. You were the only one who realized it at the time. What a fine crew you two make!"

Herbillon pressed a slightly trembling hand against his forehead. He was thinking about how his mistress, Maury's wife, was hiding behind a flimsy partition.

"Listen, Marbot… I've got a splitting headache…"

"I understand. I'm going. See you tonight?"

"Maybe."

"Have a wank, it's the best cure for a hangover."

Marbot stopped dead in his tracks. His beady eyes had just noticed a pair of women's gloves on the windowsill.

"Tell me then, is that what you call a headache? They all swoon for you, don't they? Say no more… say no more… I'm leaving. I'll leave you with this though…"

A strange sort of seriousness weighed on his podgy, jovial face, and he continued "…there is one woman you should stay away from: Maury's wife. It wouldn't be appropriate. He's one of us: we're a squadron."

The cadet went so pale in the face that Marbot grabbed him by the shoulders with deep affection.

"Forgive me, old chap," he said, "I was just joking!

I know you too well for that. You're incapable of being such a cad. Goodbye, old chap!"

As soon as Denise was able to leave the closet, Jean exclaimed, in the grips of a kind of horror: "Leave, I beg you. Did you hear all that? I don't know what I would have done if he'd seen you here."

"Where will we meet again?" she slowly asked.

"Later. Give me some time to think… Bacoli's just a village. I'll tell you tomorrow."

Denise's inflexible obstinacy, which had already terrorized Jean, reappeared on her forehead. "I can't wait until tomorrow. I have to see you, even if we have to meet in a public place."

"That's impossible, there's nowhere to go in this town except for Paméla's nightclub."

"And that's where I'll go this evening. I'll persuade Claude."

She left without kissing him, betting that he'd probably consent to her request so long as he didn't feel the touch of perfidy on his skin right away.

Herbillon showed up at the cabaret very early. The room, however, was already half full, and after quickly scanning the room, Jean immediately noticed Maury and his wife seated at a prominent table, surrounded by Doc, Marbot and Narbonne. He limited himself to waving at them from afar and called out Paméla's name, who, having quickly turning around to look at the entrance, had clearly been waiting for him. She unceremoniously left the three artillery officers she'd been talking to and submissively answered his call, beaming as she did so.

"Come have a drink with me," the cadet told her.

He felt bizarrely calm. The scene he'd most feared—seeing Maury sat next to Denise—had had completely the opposite effect he'd imagined when the thought of it had made him tremble. As is the case with all nightmares conjured by one's imagination, his completely vanished the moment he saw it right before his very eyes, in all its naked reality. He could see Maury and his bony body, his crooked shoulders, his greying hair. Then he saw Denise, with her smooth skin and little girl's face. He beheld both of them as though he owned them, by dint of their clearly defined relationships with him, which was doubtlessly cruel, but it was a human sort of cruelty nonetheless.

As soon as that realization dawned on him, in just the space of a few seconds, everything seemed possible and easy.

In a weary, imperious tone, he told Paméla: "I need you to do me a big favour. I need a place where I can have a rendezvous tomorrow afternoon."

Almost without parting her fleshy lips, the singer asked him: "An amorous rendezvous?"

Herbillon nodded his head.

"So you decided to ask me?..." Paméla queried, instantly dropping all formalities in a way she hadn't dared to do until that moment, as though the act of renunciation Herbillon had just asked of her had given her the right to do so. "Is it so you can meet the little girl who's sitting with your comrades?"

Unsurprised by her guesswork, Herbillon replied: "Yes, it's her... You're the only one who can help me. My friends must never find out about this."

Paméla glanced at Maury, then his wife, and then the cadet. A profound realization dawned on her and her face filled with great pity.

"Understood, little one," she sweetly answered. "Come back here tomorrow, but remember that my place has to be empty by six o'clock. Thanks to yesterday's kerfuffle, the cabaret has been ordered to close starting from midnight tonight."

At that precise moment, Maury stood up. He could

no longer bear the visible tension on his wife's face. He headed towards Herbillon. At which Paméla left her chair and, as though randomly wandering through the gaps left between the tables, she went straight for Denise. Pretending to fix a buckle on her shoes, she whispered in her ear: "He'll be waiting for you here tomorrow at four thirty."

Maury returned with the cadet and said: "Herbillon owes Paméla a debt of kindness; after all, it's his fault that the cabaret is being closed down."

Then, turning to his wife, he asked her: "You remember Herbillon, don't you, Hélène?"

"But of course I do!"

The young woman's answer had been completely unrestrained.

"Are you enjoying yourself in Bacoli, Madame?" Herbillon asked her.

A banal, superficial conversation ensued, which Maury analysed with every fibre of his sentient being. He failed to find any fault in it, so he felt ashamed of himself once again.

CHAPTER VIII

THE FOLLOWING DAY, Maury returned to the squadron's office after lunch and Hélène went upstairs to rest. The early July heat was oppressive.

Having carefully examined all the accounts, and the inventory records for all the rations, Maury set himself to the tedious task of writing his daily report. He'd just completed half of it when his orderly handed over an urgent parcel and a dispatch that an air force motor-cycle messenger had just delivered. Claude opened the messages, read them, then reread them, then began staring at them without actually seeing them, as though wanting to divine the unknown events they seemed to foreshadow. Then he commanded his orderly: "Take my car and bring all the officers here. As quickly as possible. Go round to all their houses and look in all the cafés. I want them all here right away!"

Maury made a great effort to banish from his mind all those new images and thoughts that had suddenly assailed him. Above all, he simply had to finish that report.

One by one, the pilots and observers entered his office. Some who'd been in the middle of their afternoon nap had hastily put some clothes on and had just barely buttoned up their jackets and tightened their belts. Others bore the traces of booze and card games on their faces. As each of them entered, Maury greeted them briefly and then resumed writing his report.

"I'll speak as soon as everyone gets here," he told the first to arrive.

In the end, Herbillon was the only one still missing. Having finished his work, Claude lifted his gaze and failed to spot him among the assembled officers. He questioned the orderly, who said he hadn't been able to find him anywhere. Even Paméla herself had assured him that she had no idea as to his whereabouts.

"Too bad," Maury said. "You'll have to fill him in later, Marbot. I can't wait any longer and I won't be here this evening. I'll be driving to pick the captain up from the station."

"Thélis is back already?" Marbot asked.

"He is; this is the telegram he sent—he had to go to the Ministry to see what the situation was like."

Claude paused very briefly, but long enough for him to guess what was going through his comrades' minds. Although they didn't know it, they had a hunch about what Maury was going to tell them. Maury continued in his smoothest, calmest tone: "The holiday's over. Tomorrow we'll leave Bacoli and head back to Château-Thierry. The Germans are going to attack along the Marne, it's the last card they've got left to play."

"They have a right to fight, don't they?" Marbot ungracefully commented, expressing what everyone else was thinking.

"I'm more reassured by Thélis's return than by the dispatch sent by HQ," Maury said.

The men who'd assembled in the squadron's office were all used to danger. However, they presently avoided each others' gazes. They were all afraid of seeing the mark of a gruesome fate etched on their comrades' faces since, by dint of their youth and habits, each and every one of them believed himself to be protected by some lucky star.

"We're going to come out of this bruised and battered," Doc said.

"That's our job!" Narbonne exclaimed, easily the most carefree of them all.

"We'll see," Marbot opined, being the most fatalistic.

"Listen up, this is the departure plan: our planes will be waiting for us in Trilport; they're all ready for us. We'll start on the road tomorrow at noon, the formations will be—"

He was interrupted by a knock on the door.

"Lieutenant," Maury's orderly began, "it's your wife…"

"No, she can't come in!" Maury exclaimed.

He turned to his comrades and apologized:

"Excuse me for a moment…"

Hélène was waiting for him in the corridor, looking so glowing, refreshed and full of life that Claude needed every iota of the absolute self-restraint he'd mastered over the course of so many years in order to keep his emotions concealed.

"So many mysteries today," the young woman exclaimed. "Are you conspiring?"

"No, we're just discussing our duties."

"Is it important?"

"No… what are you doing?"

"I just wanted to tell you that I'm going for a long walk in the countryside, the heat's died down a little now… don't worry if I come back a little late."

"That's no problem at all. I have to go on a long drive and I'm afraid I might even have to miss out on dinner."

The pleasure she felt at knowing she had so much free time at her disposal prevented her from asking any more questions.

"Until this evening then, darling," she said, more tenderly than usual.

"See you then! Enjoy your walk."

He kissed her in his usual manner, almost furtively so. When it was time to part, he added: "If you happen to cross paths with Herbillon, please send him over to me."

Without giving her the time to reply or even looking at her, Maury opened the door to his office.

Hélène started to move towards him, then stopped and lingered, dumbfounded. Suddenly, the voices of Maury's orderly and aide-de-camp as they left the officers' meeting pulled her out of her reverie.

"Life's so rotten!" the first said. "It was so nice being here."

"We've got nothing to moan about old chap; we'll be on the ground; think of those poor pilots. They'll go down in flames!" the other retorted.

"Life's so rotten!" the first repeated.

Hélène looked at her watch. Her precious time was slipping through her fingers, but she felt she could not leave without knowing. She sat down on a scruffy chair close to the window. She could see a calm little garden through that window. Hélène looked at it anxiously. The humming of conversations could occasionally be heard through the wall. The young woman listened worriedly in vain.

The officers left the office, greeting Hélène Maury distractedly as they went out into the street in silence. Marbot and Doc were the last people left in the room with Claude. When they finally appeared on the threshold, the young woman almost shoved past them to get in.

"Why did you choose not to tell me you'd be going back to the front?" she exclaimed.

Maury didn't waste any time in asking her how she'd found out.

"I wanted to tell you," he sweetly told her, "but first I had to give the others their orders."

"So, it's going to happen soon?"

"Very..."

"When?"

He hesitated.

"Tomorrow?" the young woman murmured.

"Yes… at noon."

As soon as he'd uttered those words, Claude felt a great sense of peace swell within him. He felt as though the difficult part was already behind him. The front was already taking over his life. The torments he would face alongside the peril of war hadn't yet entered his consciousness. Herbillon… their painful partnership… all that belonged to the world of men. For now, his only concern was that face ravaged by concern and those intense eyes which he badly wanted to reassure. Up until that moment, Claude had never realized how much he loved Hélène, or how selfless that love really was. He took her hands in his and caressed them. All of a sudden, he felt her cold, stiff hands clench his.

"Why are you so panic-stricken?" Claude asked with as sincere a smile as he could manage. "We won't be in any more danger there than—"

"That's not true," Hélène interrupted him. "I heard the orderlies and I saw your comrades' faces, and they're certainly not cowards."

Maury made a gesture of helplessness.

"Claude," the young woman cried, swept away in a sort of delirium. "Claude, I don't want… put a stop to this, you're in charge here… massacres, men being burned alive… it's unacceptable, unforgivable!… You, the others… charred remains… I don't want that… I can't stand that…"

She sought his shoulder and pressed herself tightly against him. Although Claude was torn apart by the spectacle of that pain, he also felt strong and safe, because he believed it was all for his sake.

He lifted the head that was buried in his chest and spoke like a hypnotist: "Listen to me, and listen to me closely. Nothing will happen to us, I promise you. I'll be careful and vigilant, don't worry."

He carried on in this manner for a while, as long as she kept staring at him incredulously like a lost child.

The phone rang. Maury picked up the receiver and, after a few moments, replied: "Surely not, Colonel, just think, we're going back to the front tomorrow."

He hung up and, glad for the diversion, shrugged his shoulders and explained: "They're all crazy over there at headquarters. They want me to send a volunteer to be an instructor at Fontainebleau. On the eve of a major attack!"

Hélène leaned against the desk, which was stacked full of papers. The room started spinning in front of her eyes.

"What are you saying?" she stammered. "An instructor for the rear… safety?"

Maury stopped her with a gesture which he tried to inject with all his tenderness, and his voice quivered with recognition as he told her: "No, that would just be impossible, don't even think about it, please."

He stopped abruptly. He could see the signs of a profound hatred invade his wife's features.

"So you'll never stop playing heroes!" she said as she left, without looking back.

Claude didn't try to stop her, or to catch up to her. He barely had enough time to go pick up Thélis. Besides, what could Hélène possibly add to the terror she'd already expressed for his sake?

CHAPTER IX

HERBILLON HAD shown up at Paméla's far earlier than he'd needed to, eager to seek shelter in the only place where he felt safe.

The singer led him into a place she called a retiring room. With its thick cotton curtains, armchairs upholstered in rep and a Louis Philippe sofa, it had retained the aspect of a sitting room forgotten by time.

There were still some soldiers playing cards in the main room. Herbillon distractedly listened to the noise as it gradually started to die down. He didn't want to let his thoughts wander freely.

When Paméla came to tell him that she'd sent Maury's orderly away, he hadn't felt anxious in the slightest. Claude, thorough as ever, had no doubt wanted to discuss some trivial matter with him. Herbillon continued to wait, his mind perfectly at ease, as though it had frozen still.

Some light footsteps crunched along the garden's gravel path. Denise burst in panting and exclaimed:

"You're leaving tomorrow! You're going back to the front!"

Herbillon felt a wonderful sense of joy flow through his veins. That enchanted, infernal circle had broken up of its own accord! Everything had quickly and easily resolved itself! He was afraid he'd misunderstood her.

"Are you sure? Are you sure?" he asked her, his face beaming with a restrained elation that was nonetheless ready to burst.

"Claude told me; it's dreadful..."

The officer cadet burst out in a laugh that made Denise shudder.

"You didn't really think we were going to spend the rest of the war in Bacoli, did you darling?"

He drew close to her in order to kiss her, but she violently shoved him away.

"Listen to me, you're going to be part of an offensive. You'll be in danger day and night. Three quarters of your squadron won't make it back alive."

"We'll see about that... why waste our time thinking about something we can do nothing about? You're here... I'm happy."

"Just for a single night! Is that enough for you?" Denise shouted. "So once you've got rid of me, you'll be satisfied and calm? You'll be with your dear comrades, rejoin your beloved squadron, go flying with your friend Claude..."

The young woman's features betrayed such scathing sarcasm that Herbillon didn't pay much attention to her last words and instead, looking at her attentively, he asked: "Do you really think you're right, Denise? Do you think I had any say in this departure, which I only just learned from your lips anyway? Haven't you noticed that I've sacrificed everything for you?"

"So stay!"

Herbillon wrapped his hands around his mistress's face and stroked it.

"Come now, darling, come back to your senses. Would you really rather they shot me as a deserter?"

Denise freed her face from his hands, stared pointedly at him and said: "When I was in the office, Claude received a phone call from headquarters asking for a volunteer instructor to teach at Fontainebleau."

"And?" Herbillon asked, failing to grasp her meaning.

Denise didn't answer him, but her gaze grew more intense.

"Oh! Denise..." Herbillon murmured. "You didn't really think? Did you?... Could you really... think I'd go hide in some cushy posting? Ask Claude to send me to the school, while Thélis and all the others take part in that offensive? Oh! You'd have to be a woman to come up with something so filthy!"

The young woman's face beamed with a magnificent humility.

"Keep insulting me as much as you like, Jean… but stay. I don't have a code of honour; you're the only thing I have in this world. My dear Jean, I don't want you to be hit by bullets, for the fire to burn you."

She was so beautiful and so clearly full of sorrow that Jean forgave her.

"I can't just abandon my comrades," he told her sweetly.

"I love you," Denise replied.

"What would Thélis say?"

"I love you," the young woman repeated.

Herbillon decided to adopt a line of argument that would matter to her as much as it did to him.

"Maury would be in greater danger without me."

Denise didn't lower her gaze, and kept it fixed on him, raising her voice until it sounded fierce and almost cruel: "I love you," she repeated.

Herbillon looked at Denise and felt strange. He didn't think he had much in common with this maniac, whose entire reasoning and logic were encapsulated in those three words. Jean started to hate those words. Did loving someone give one the absolute right to decide how they should live or die? Was there a more tyrannical law she could invoke?

"Well, no!" Herbillon viciously declared. "I won't let Maury fight without me!"

Denise breathed in some air in a hopeless manner and then stressed each word: "The entire squadron—and not just Claude—is going to learn of our last night together in Paris. You want to leave? You prize their esteem above anything else? At least they'll know you for who you really are. It's been far too easy for you to have me as your mistress and then keep flying with Claude and for your comrades to think of you as one of their own as though nothing had happened. I'm ready to pay the price for my love. So you should pay for yours and give up your crew."

A series of images flashed through Herbillon's mind. The squadron's hostility, Thélis's disgust… Denise always kept her word. He was sure she would carry out her threat.

"I'll ask for the transfer this evening," he murmured.

A happy cry sprang from her loins and reached his ears: "Jean, Jean, you're saved!"

Denise stammered, prayed, laughed, cried and praised all at the same time: "I'll make you forget everything… we'll be happy… you won't regret it…"

Herbillon nodded, forcing a vague shameful smile as she wrapped her loving, maternal arms around him. From this moment on he had accepted everything. There were two accomplices in that dimly lit room, and this was no longer a betrayal, but a crime.

Denise was still flinging her incoherent words at Jean when Paméla burst into the room: "Get out of here, get out of here, leave through the garden door."

If Herbillon had had his usual wits about him, he would have grabbed Denise in time, but they'd both just been through a very intense argument. They lost a few seconds loosening out of their embrace and trying to understand what was going on. But by then it was too late. The unit of policemen dispatched to ascertain whether Paméla had obeyed her instructions to close her nightclub surprised them in the room. It was led by the very officer whom Herbillon had humiliated.

"They're just friends of mine," Paméla exclaimed. "You can see that they're not drinking. Leave us alone."

"Your papers," the policeman asked.

Shrugging his shoulders, the officer cadet held out his military passbook.

"And yours, Madame."

"I'll answer for her," Herbillon said. "Please don't insist."

"Your permit papers, Madame? This is a war zone; our orders are very specific."

Denise obeyed, without the slightest embarrassment.

"Madame Hélène Maury," the policeman said softly as he wrote her name down next to the cadet's. "Thank you."

Then he turned to Herbillon.

"I'm giving you two minutes to clear out of here."

He went back to his men, who were waiting for him in the larger room. Herbillon made to stop him, but Denise held him back firmly by the arm, saying:

"What does it matter now?"

Denise and Herbillon left Bacoli behind and walked for a long time. First the twilight and then the darkness cast their shroud over their joyless, aimless flight through the fields and meadows. Herbillon wanted to go back to Bacoli as late as possible. He already felt as though the squadron had banished him, and he trembled at the thought that he might run into a comrade. Having bent him to her will, Denise went with him to ensure she kept exercising her influence over him.

By the time they found themselves in front of the house where the squadron's office and Maury's rooms were located, like two barely distinguishable shadows, the officer cadet felt nothing except a boundless weariness and a burning desire to leave this shameful stop on his journey behind and head forth towards his new destiny.

It was very late at night, but there was a light in one of the ground-floor windows.

"Maury's still working. All the better. I'll go speak to him now."

Denise pressed herself against the young man, without saying a word, then began climbing the stairs that led to Claude's room. She stopped halfway up. She looked through the darkness at the bright space engulfing Herbillon.

When he stepped inside, the officer cadet resolved to stick to the two or three sentences that the situation required. Everything had to take place using the cool, artificial tone that he and Maury had conversed in for some time now, which would allow them to avoid all arguments, making the confession of the ultimate crime he'd committed pass without incident, in so far as it was possible.

Yet as soon as he'd crossed the office threshold, Herbillon was frightened to see Thélis sitting right next to Maury. They were examining some papers.

The captain raised his head and his gaze stopped the friendly way in which Herbillon—despite everything—still moved.

"Here you are, finally…" the captain said, his voice devoid of any of the usually benevolent inflections Herbillon so dearly loved. "We're leaving tomorrow, you know that, right?"

"Precisely… I wanted…" the cadet stammered, "to talk to Maury about this… but since you're back, Captain…"

"I'm listening."

"I would prefer to speak to you privately, Captain."

"Is it regarding an order?"

"That's right."

"So speak to Maury. He's still in charge of the squadron."

Herbillon said, with a lump in his throat: "I would like to formally request to be posted as this squadron's volunteer instructor at Fontainebleau."

Not a single muscle moved on Thélis's face. Yet his beautiful golden eyes grew wider and hardened, as though he'd just been dealt an unwarranted insult.

"I never thought any of my men would volunteer," he said, slowly, "but it's your right to ask for it."

"Thank you, Captain," Herbillon murmured.

He took a step towards the door. Claude stopped him.

"Allow me to ask you how you learned of the existence of this post," he said. "I didn't put up an official notice anywhere as I thought it would be pointless. In addition, you've been gone all afternoon."

"Indeed…" Herbillon desperately replied. "Indeed… I met a comrade from headquarters. He was the one who…"

Even someone without a reason to suspect him would have realized that Jean's features and voice betrayed the fact he was was lying. The truth was so atrociously obvious to Claude that he forgot Thélis and Herbillon were still in the room. His wife's distraught features and her sudden fears and hopes flashed across his mind again… and those marvellous gifts which he'd naively, grotesquely thought had been intended for him, were instead meant for Herbillon. Because only Hélène—and Maury knew this better than anyone else—could have told the officer cadet about the post. A kind of evil pulsed in Maury's temples; the air felt choked inside his hollow chest. He stood up, albeit with difficulty.

"You're tired, Maury," Thélis told him. "I'll finish up on my own here. Be at the car park by nine tomorrow."

The captain watched Maury leave, then, without looking at Jean, he ordered him: "Write up your transfer request, quickly, I don't have any time to lose."

Herbillon sat down and picked up a sheet of paper. Thélis walked in large strides across the room. As though about to undertake a superhuman task, the officer cadet painfully started to write. The pen's creaks made the captain's impassive face twitch. He stopped walking and started staring at Herbillon's head.

It was young and strong, just like the rest of the cadet's body, and was settled atop his strong, loyal shoulders; and yet there it was bowed down by so much weariness and humiliation… a brotherly tenderness lit up the captain's hardened face. He wasn't going to give up on his cadet without a fight.

"Herbillon," he suddenly said, "I promise to do everything I can to ensure that the comrades think you were appointed to the post against your will."

The cadet's fingers began to tremble so hard that he couldn't finish the word he'd been shaping. Thélis continued in his sharp, friendly voice: "Maury won't say a word. I'll ask him not to."

The cadet dropped his pen and half-turned to face the captain but, although he moved his lips, he wasn't able to make a sound.

"That way," Thélis concluded, "everyone in the squadron will miss you."

"Captain, Captain… listen…"

Herbillon was unable to continue. Big, raw, manly sobs choked him up, while a furious inner revolt tore him apart and crumbled the question he'd failed to ask into pieces.

"Please don't judge me, Captain," he moaned. "It's not that I'm afraid; if only you knew…"

Thélis ran his hand through the cadet's hair.

"I know," he said, with a kindness his comrades wouldn't have thought him capable of.

Herbillon lifted his feverish, bewildered gaze to face the captain.

"The police report on the events that transpired at Paméla's today just arrived. I got back just in time."

A very long silence ensued.

"Go get some sleep," the captain ordered him.

*

Claude walked up the staircase, feeling his breath between each step. During that long climb, he had all the time he needed to recompose himself. Yet he had been dealt such a devastatingly violent blow that his wife on seeing him had exclaimed: "My god Claude, are you ill?" The sincerity of her concern prevented him from speaking. Hélène was showing concern for him, which of course was nothing like that raw horror she'd displayed a few hours earlier, but which was nevertheless tender and attentive. The habit of reassuring her that he'd acquired suddenly kicked in, despite his own suffering and the fact his inner world had completely collapsed in on him.

"It's nothing," he said. "I've just been overworked while trying to finalize all the preparations for our departure tomorrow. I would make quite a poor squadron commander."

Having already given in to one of his habits, Maury couldn't help succumbing to yet another, which proved even more urgent than the first: that of understanding, which would inevitably lead to him justifying it too.

His wife's attitude helped him in that regard. She'd bent her frail, naked shoulders and fragile innocent neck towards him.

After all, was it Hélène's fault if, being so young, she

had fallen in love with youth itself? If Herbillon's charm, courage and kindness—whose allure Claude knew all too well—had had such a powerful influence on Hélène, whom he'd deprived of those qualities simply by marrying her? Wasn't it also quite natural that Herbillon would have fallen in love with his wife, who knew no equal? Wasn't it only natural that he was the one who brought them together?

Claude was old enough and experienced enough not to hate Herbillon for having been so weak, nor did he judge him. Perhaps if Hélène had been able to love him with such fierceness, then he might have done exactly what Jean did…

Maury had reached such a degree of selflessness and universal compassion that it was like an agonizing sort of bliss. He wanted to travel down that road as far as it would lead him.

"I think Herbillon won't be leaving with us," he said. "He found out about the post from some comrade of his and he asked Thélis to be posted there."

"What did the captain say?" his young wife asked.

"He accepted his request. He couldn't have done otherwise."

Hélène stayed silent. What could she possibly say that wouldn't betray her happiness?

"I'm going to sleep on the sofa in the next room," Claude murmured. "I have to get up early tomorrow, and I don't want to wake you up."

As she watched her husband leave, more clumsily than ever, Hélène experienced such shame that she thought she was burning on the inside. But she'd wanted her victory so badly, and so fiercely fought for it, to let this make a dent in it.

"Claude… he'll recover," she thought to herself, in a falsely reassuring way.

The young woman was busy packing her suitcase when the captain had his presence announced. "I'm happy to make your acquaintance," Hélène Maury said. "Claude and his comrades have spoken so highly of you."

Thélis observed her closely, and Hélène felt overcome with a slight unease, although she couldn't discern its origins.

"You're looking for Claude, right?" she continued. "He isn't here."

"I know where he is—he's in the car park," Thélis said. "I'm here in regards to Herbillon."

"I don't understand…" she mumbled.

Thélis carried on quickly, as though he hadn't heard her: "You must forgive me, Madame, I've only come here because I felt that I had to. I know about everything… yes, about everything. Please listen to me."

"Did Jean?…"

"No, it was the police patrol that saw you last night."

The young woman took a deep breath and defiantly declared: "So it doesn't matter. Jean's safe."

"Indeed he is," Thélis said without changing his tone, "but not in the way you think…"

The captain noticed the young woman withdraw into herself, giving her body a feline quiver, showing she was ready to defend herself and, imperceptibly shaking his head, he said: "Don't look on me as your enemy. It's too late."

"What do you mean?" Hélène cried. "Did you take him back into the squadron?"

"I didn't—and neither did anyone else. It was his own choice."

"It's not true… it's impossible. You refused his request. You have no right to do that."

"He didn't give me the chance to refuse it. He tore the request up right in front of my eyes."

"After all the promises he made… after… and I even believed him, I even believed that he loved me."

"Oh, he loves you! You can rest assured about that," Thélis said. "In fact, even more than I thought possible."

The young woman replied with a laugh that was a little too shrill and obsessive: "Sure, he loves me, but he's going to stay…"

The captain's face betrayed curiousness and incredulity: "Did you really think you could drag him away? Ask him to deny…"

"Deny what? The squadron?… You?… His honour?… *The crew*! Spare me your speeches. They won't work on me. He's going to meet his death and is going to leave me behind, when I'm the one who loves him… I'll never understand it, or allow it, or forgive him for it, never!"

Contrary to what Herbillon had done, Thélis didn't try to plead with her or convince her. He was too wise and clear-sighted not to understand that a real, genuine woman—and the one standing in front of him was a shining example of that particular breed—was ruled by different stars than the ones that governed his own life, and that those stars were irreconcilable. A woman like her could suffer the rule of men under duress, but there would always be some essential part of her that would never accept it.

At that moment, the captain tried to reach out to her in order to achieve the two-fold task that had led him to talk to her: first to avoid the outburst her suffering would ensure she would cause; and secondly, to prevent Jean from returning to the front ravaged by the sorrow and resentment he'd leave behind in his wake.

Without allowing the young woman to begin pleading or complaining, he said: "Don't regret that you've failed. By following you, Herbillon would have simultaneously destroyed all his feelings for you."

"Come on!" Hélène cried out with the same twitchy laugh she'd made a few moments earlier. "Fine then! Away with you, I should have known…"

Thélis interrupted her with his voice, which was more persuasive and self-assured: "You're deceiving yourself! Try to understand, don't blind yourself to the truth. Think: without his comrades, without the call to action and the risks that come with it, Herbillon would have had nothing to distract him. He would be constantly stuck in his own thoughts. At which point he would fully comprehend his weakness. Every morning and every evening, the papers would bring him news of the front, news of us, stoking his sense of shame, aggravating his self-loathing. All of which would make him turn on you, since you would be the cause of all his dilemmas and the sole witness of his downfall. He would start to hate you…"

"Enough! Please… enough," the young woman suddenly cried.

She feebly raised her hands, as though to shield herself. Yet it was no longer the captain's voice she heard, but that of her own doubts, her own fears, which she'd barely subdued during the sleepless night she'd just experienced. She knew Herbillon far too well not to have suspected that she risked destroying his love simply by saving his life.

"Herbillon would never forgive you," the captain continued. "Moreover, as soon as a woman who knew nothing about him or the fact he'd abandoned his comrades crossed his path, someone whose mere presence wouldn't mercilessly remind him of all of that, he would leave you for her… he would fall in love with her thanks to all the hatred for you that would have grown inside him, and which he would then continue to harbour for the rest of his life…"

"So you reached the same conclusion," Denise exclaimed. "I beg you, please be blunt with me. Don't try to console me, the situation is far too serious for that. Do you really think this is what would happen?"

"I swear on the lives of the men of my squadron," the captain told her.

The young woman's arms fell limp and inert by her sides.

"So, all is well then," she murmured, her eyes having grown vacant, almost glassy.

She didn't hear Thélis leave the room.

The cars, trucks and tractors were lined up on the right side of the street that led west out of Bacoli. The sweat-drenched drivers were giving the hand cranks a few final turns to start their cars' unruly engines. The inhabitants of that little village were exchanging their final goodbyes with the officers they knew. Young female workers were smiling at the soldiers.

Maury slipped out of his wife's embrace.

"Make sure you write to me every day, Claude," she said. "I'm so afraid."

"You shouldn't be," Claude told her. "We're used to it, you know that, and with Herbillon as my observer, all the odds are in our favour."

An orderly came to inform Maury that the captain was waiting for him in the car. Maury drew close to Hélène again and they exchanged a silent kiss. Walking away in his gangly strides, Maury went to join Thélis.

The young woman started to walk back to the top of that long row of vehicles. All she wanted was to see Herbillon's face. She hadn't managed to see the cadet after her conversation with Thélis. She was scared of what she might do and that, despite herself, she might make one last attempt to persuade him to stay with her. She'd continually postponed the hour of farewell, and now that the departure was upon her, she was drained of all strength and resolve.

Herbillon suddenly emerged out of the side of the road.

"Denise, finally!" he exclaimed. "I looked around for you all morning, you were hiding from me, weren't you? But I couldn't… I just couldn't… Forgive me…"

Denise's eyes brimmed with tears, but not the sort she'd feared. They were sweet, benevolent and merciful, because they sprang from a love that came of selfless oblivion, if only for a moment.

"My poor little one…" she murmured. "Go ahead, since that's what you want, since you feel that you must. I won't make you suffer, don't worry…"

If she'd ever wanted a reward for her words, she found it in the joy and gratitude expressed by Herbillon's beaming face, which now suddenly looked as it once had: boyish, virile, eager to laugh and live.

"You're so brave, such a great person! I love you, I love you, until we meet again…"

As his car had driven past him, Herbillon had to run in order to catch it on the fly. Standing on the footboard, he cheerfully waved goodbye to his mistress. She didn't see him. She had shut her eyes.

By the time she reopened them, the trucks were already rolling past and bouncing heavily along the potholed road. Soon enough, the convoy was enshrouded by a thick veil of dust.

CHAPTER X

THEY WERE WELCOMED back to the front by the sound of artillery fire. The distant roar, which called out to them and threatened them, lent all their words and gestures a solemn depth. The tents turned the entire landscape an unblemished white; each tent housed a crew.

Entering his own tent, where two camp beds had been set up side by side, Herbillon mused over how his physical intimacy with Maury was only likely to grow. However, this wasn't the time for personal problems. One had to save one's strength for the tasks presaged by the deafening rumble on the horizon.

Herbillon ran into Thélis, who'd just returned from the new headquarters. Never had the young man seen the captain's face look so beautiful. The fire in his eyes and his body's vitality betrayed the joy caused by the exertion and the fighting.

"How lucky I've been," Thélis exclaimed, "to come

back from my leave only to stumble onto such a great undertaking!"

Finding his own enthusiasm reflected in the cadet's emotions, he asked: "Are you happy now, greenhorn?"

Then, he grew suddenly serious: "Keep your eyes peeled," he advised. "You still haven't seen what a war zone looks like."

A great shadow fell over his face, as though a premonition had just allowed him to witness the wholesale massacre of his comrades. He spoke so shyly that Herbillon barely recognized his voice: "I need you to remember something, Herbillon. I'm very religious, and if I don't come back, make sure you all say mass for me."

Without giving the young man the opportunity to reply, he ran over to his plane. Then he left, flying the first reconnaissance mission over the front lines.

By the time he returned, the light had slowly started to fade. A table was set up in the open air, and they dined on canned food, since the cook would only arrive the following day. During the meal, Thélis handed out all the assignments. Two planes would have to fly out every morning to observe the enemy's advance; another three would go out to take photographs, while two more would go out on evening patrols. Finally, a crew would be kept on permanent standby in order to fly off on urgent missions at a moment's notice.

Herbillon and Maury went on their monitoring mission a day before they had been scheduled to on the roster. Charensole and Brûlard never made it back the previous night.

The cadet wandered around the field that had been unceremoniously cleared through the bales of honey-coloured crops and thought about the missions he'd already flown over the new front. They had been mostly calm, save for the dangerously precise shots fired by an artillery battery lying in wait next to the Marne. Yet the latent danger that snapped at their heels had reinforced the bond between Herbillon and Maury more than ever before, allowing them to simultaneously share the same reflexes and know the other's thoughts and emotions.

Herbillon had figured out that Maury's suspicions had reached a point where anything seemed possible. His logic had run aground on what he still thought was a physical impossibility, yet he no longer doubted his instincts; and the young man discerned a frightening certitude in Claude that even the latter was probably oblivious to, but which caused him a sadness that spread over his face and made him look like a mortally wounded animal.

The sight of a plane's shadow on the ground pulled him out of his reverie. Virense and Michel had just returned. The smoothness of the landing was a testament to the pilot's technique. Jean headed towards the plane to question his comrades. Nevertheless, neither of them left the cockpit. Herbillon called out to them, but they didn't reply. Slightly worried, he jumped up on the footboard and let out a cry. The rudder, leather cushion and interiors were drenched in blood, and Virense was slumped back in his seat, his eyes shut. The young man's gaze shifted to the observer's cockpit, where a pile of human remains lay on the floor.

Faced with the sight of that sinister plane, which had seemingly returned only to deliver a couple of corpses, Herbillon started to tremble.

They later learned that despite having had his right wrist shattered by shrapnel, Virense had had the strength to land his corpse-bearing plane, but had fainted the moment the wheels had touched the ground.

Narbonne, who was scheduled to fly next, frowned and grumbled: "A bumpy ride."

Narbonne firmly believed—and his overall experiences had merely reaffirmed that belief—that death, just like a game of chance, liked to work according to sequences. Nevertheless, he made a cheerful gesture towards Sorgues, the machine gunner, who climbed into the plane with him.

An hour went by. All of a sudden, Jean shuddered and raised his head. Although he couldn't spot anything in the sky, which was enveloped in a thin mist, a faint crackling resounded through the air.

"Maury!" the young man yelled.

Claude ran out of his tent and shouted: "Yes, they're fighting up there!"

They stood and listened for a few seconds. Machine guns were being fired aboard invisible planes. They exchanged a look.

Claude hesitated.

"They must be at least five miles up in the air," he said. "We won't reach them in time."

He'd scarcely finished talking when Jean grabbed his hand and pressed it until it hurt.

"It's over," he murmured.

A spark fell out of the sky, yet it did so from such heights that Maury doubted it for a moment longer. It began growing vertiginously: a bird in flames, a ball of fire, a burning plane.

A group of pilots and mechanics left their tents.

"French?" they yelled.

"Yes, a Salmson."

"Chased right down to the ground."

"One of ours?"

"Narbonne."

"He's not crashing, he's just nosediving of his own accord, he's still alive."

Overcome with a helpless anguish, they were forced to look on while their comrade attempted to exploit the velocity of his breakneck drop to land the plane before it burst into flames. They pictured him rammed against his vertical rudder, running his engine at full speed, gripped by his furious desire to plunge his plane into the field close to where the charred fuselage of the previous plane that had gone up before it had landed.

Words no longer bound by reason punctuated that desperate fight.

"So long as the wings hold steady!"

"You can hear the engine!"

"There he is, right above us!"

"Make way! Make way!"

But nobody budged. The winged fireball was now only a dozen or so metres above the ground, and all their thoughts were focused on that horrible landing, when a clamour suddenly rose up: "He's going to jump!"

A burning mass leaped out and crashed on the ground. At the same time, the burning plane hit the adjacent wheat field with a resounding thud until it lay half-buried in the earth.

Herbillon and Maury were the first to rush towards the pilot. They found nothing there except a giant, blistered mass. The skin had slipped off his body in strips, leaving only blackened flesh in its wake. All the features on that swollen face had melted together into a lumpy pile of fat. Neither Claude nor Jean could recognize their comrade, and the horror they felt refused to leave any room for pity.

The same shudder ran through them. The shapeless mass, which bore no correlation to the man they'd watched fly off just an hour earlier, suddenly emitted a voice, a familiar voice, the same voice they'd heard resonate through the mess hall, or during a game of cards as it had laughed so candidly. Far from being delirious, it sounded lucidly conscious; and although its lips were nothing but a swollen mess, that broken, monstrous stranger was employing Narbonne's voice to utter its final words.

Later that day, the army corps entrusted the emergency standby crew to photograph the bridges over the river Marne.

The mission was going to be the most dangerous of all. Thélis, who had just returned from the front and whose brow was furrowed in a painful rage, resolved to fly out alongside Doc in order to provide Claude some cover.

The three planes quickly crossed over into enemy skies. Maury scanned ahead and turned to face Herbillon. A single look synchronized their faculties. Their ability to choose the right timing to engage over the Marne would determine their mission's success, as well as their own fate. Their plane would have to keep the same speed and altitude as it flew from Dormans to Château-Thierry in order to ensure the consistency of their photographs. They also had to make sure that German fighter planes wouldn't come up behind them during their flight.

For one last time, the cadet's eyes attentively scanned the sky without noticing anything suspicious. There were some clouds above the Vesle that could easily be concealing enemy aircraft, but as he didn't want to prolong what was already a dangerous wait, Jean gestured to Claude; the plane slowly began to veer. The escort planes behind them faithfully copied their movements.

The river's blue course appeared through the bull's eye underneath the cadet's feet. Jean retracted his head inside the cockpit and entrusted his fate to Maury. Manoeuvring the gigantic camera which usually hampered his freedom of movement now took up the entirety of his efforts.

The river Marne slithered along under his eyes. Jean pulled the camera's trigger and replaced the plates in clockwork motions. The image of Denise inevitably forced its way into his mind. He would have liked her to see him now, clever and alert, surrounded by mortal dangers, carrying out a mission that could ensure their victory.

Inside the forward cockpit, his fingers wrapped tightly around the rudder, keeping his ear focused on the engine's aspirations, his eyes going back and forth between the control dials and the sky, Maury was thinking about the same woman.

Both men—two souls inside a single body—linked their knowledge and clairvoyance to successfully accomplish the same task. They'd made one another suffer, even hated each other at times, while their senses and nerves, which were bound so tightly together, like the plane's control dials, worked in unison. They were the intelligent cogs of the fragile, powerful machine they were flying in, and the same fluid ran through their veins.

A mysterious warning shot distracted Jean from his work. The plane dived.

The perfidious clouds lit up with sombre sparks. It was twelve German planes, but at first glance Jean noticed they were not in any immediate danger; Claude had anticipated the attack well in advance and the German planes hadn't moved quickly enough to pursue them.

Nevertheless, the joy prompted by that feeling of safety evaporated soon enough. Thélis and Doc had refused to abandon the plane they were escorting, and since they were still above the Marne, the German fighter planes quickly fell upon them, coming down on them like a powerful stream, while the two planes veered south. But it didn't take long for the fastest single-seater aeroplanes to be on their tails.

A feeling of dread took a hold of the young man as he confronted that swarm of wild wasps hell-bent on murder. He hesitated for just a second, although it seemed longer than the span of a painful life. He had avoided that danger, and joining the fight now would almost certainly mean death. Finally waking up to the reality of danger, he felt afraid, miserably so.

Maury turned towards him and waited for him to make up his mind, respecting the strict code whereby the observer decided the crew's fate. At which point Jean *listened* to Maury's thoughts. At first he felt Claude was as indecisive as he was; then he felt him free himself from his cowardice, ready to do whatever he could to help his comrades.

He raised his hand in the direction of where the dogfight was taking place and suddenly, reversing its course, the plane climbed towards the patch of sky crisscrossed by incandescent bullets.

The young man's fears evaporated. He stopped thinking. His blank mind transmitted mechanical orders to the rest of his body. He checked the magazines of his machine guns, and the flexibility of his turret. A winged shape leaped under his eyes, quickly followed by others. He started shooting, in little rapid, regular busts, just like they'd taught him at the academy. Claude's machine gun echoed his efforts.

It was only once he landed that he was able to reconstruct the scene: surprised by the attack, the German fighter planes swayed and hesitated long enough to allow Thélis to slip free, and then Maury happily manoeuvred away and escaped. At the time, all he'd seen had been a plane bearing black crosses on its wings plummet like a stone towards the Marne, at which he'd thought: "I shot it down."

The last he saw of it was when it was only a few feet from the ground, while the rest of the German patrol headed west.

Claude's eyes were still pinned on him, questioningly so. They still hadn't completed their mission. They'd only taken half the photographs they'd been asked for. Herbillon listened to the engine's cheerful buzz. There were no mechanical reasons to prevent them from carrying out the task they'd been forced to interrupt. Yet their escort planes were no longer there and the German patrol hadn't quite disappeared over the horizon.

However, Jean *felt* the same irrepressible desire well up within both of them. He removed the empty clips from his guns and replaced them with new ones. Maury didn't require any further indication and he headed towards the river.

They climbed back up to the altitude they'd reached before the attack and, starting from Château-Thierry, they hugged the Marne in the opposite direction. At the same time that Jean spied the ruined bridge, the result of his emptied clips, through his bull's eye, the enemy patrol headed back towards them. Nevertheless, they were too far behind to catch up to them, and soon enough the tents of their camp came into view. However, Herbillon only felt safe once he finally saw the shadow of their plane form on the ground.

Thélis, who'd been waiting for them, ran up to them and hugged them passionately. When he finally realized they'd completed their mission unescorted, he said: "I don't know if I would have taken such a risk."

The two men felt this was a worthier prize than any they could have imagined.

The captain continued to gaze at them emotionally and continued: "Maury, Herbillon," he said. "There's been a lot of bad blood between you for some time now, but if you don't want to spoil my day, please hug one another."

This time, Claude was the one who turned away.

After having cut its numbers down to half over the space of only a few days, fate spared the squadron any further losses. However, the remaining crewmen struggled on only by dint of an effort that pushed them beyond the normal limits of human endurance. Only Thélis was able to lead by example and keep his overworked men's spirits high, after the latter's minds were clouded by the sombre forebodings prompted by their comrades' deaths.

Thélis flew all the time, took part in every mission, only stopping long enough to change planes, taking up the new observers who'd come to replace the one who'd perished: boys who made up for their inexperience with their unparalleled skills and unwavering bravery. No prayer or warning could hold him back. Thélis was at a level of exhaustion that he only managed to overcome through sheer fanaticism. People said that he flew so he could get drunk on danger and fatigue, and thus forget the ongoing massacre, to keep death's eyes focused on him alone.

He eventually succeeded.

One morning, piloted by an unsteady hand, a plane crashed its landing gear against a road embankment in the countryside around Meaux.

The crash occurred during that ambivalent time of day when the last shadows of the summer night still break through the dawn's light, allowing one to feel its smoothness. An enormous, pensive sort of peace closed back around the track where the plane had pierced through the stillness of the air.

Marbot's massive shadow emerged out of the rear cockpit. A red streak ran down his shoulder. He climbed down with difficulty and headed towards the forward cockpit. As the engine had broken off and had sagged to the ground, Marbot was able to stick his head up so it was level with the aperture, where the captain's helmet was still visible.

"Thélis," he weakly groaned. "Thélis, old chap."

He wasn't at all surprised that he couldn't hear the voice of the man he was calling out to. Approaching collapse, Marbot leaned against the edge of the cockpit. Blurry, muddled snapshots that summed up the last three years they'd spent fighting and laughing together flashed past his eyes, juxtaposed against memories of physical pain.

Their first flight, when Thélis had still been a pilot officer… when he'd had a sore neck… the night they'd drunk an entire cellar's worth of champagne… when his head had spun and ached… the time the captain's voice had sounded sharper than a bugle… when his legs had trembled… and by the time the image of Thélis laughing as he climbed into his plane went by, Marbot finally fainted…

Time went by. The confused heap of scrap the plane had transformed into emerged out of the dawn light. Thélis felt the horizontal rudder pushing against his chest. Slouched against his seat, he stood up and the sun's first fiery rays overwhelmed him. With gestures he no longer had any control over, he removed his furs, which were stifling him, and then, using the little strength still left in him, he tumbled out of the cockpit onto the nearby earth.

Once there, his feet stumbled onto a torso. Thélis fell on his knees and whispered: "Ah, it's you, Marbot, come on, get up."

Silence hung over the plane again. Clinging to the plane's fuselage, Thélis stood up straight and lingered motionless for a moment. His parched lips sucked some air in, making him wheeze.

The captain slowly and dimly began to understand he was still alive; he remembered nothing of the fight except the sounds the dying engine had made and the shock of impact. He started to walk, without a specific aim in mind. He simply wanted to flee the remains of that shattered plane, as well as his comrade's body, and the smell of the blood that had spilled all around him.

The tranquility of the fields ahead tempted him towards them. He was unable to think about anything. He felt his heart murmur inside him like a sickly insect. The dawn air helped his muscles stretch, and each time he moved, he felt a deceptive lightness that made him stumble with every step he took. As he no longer exercised any control over his body, his arms surprised him as they tried to keep him balanced, albeit ineffectively. Sometimes, he even sat down, without knowing that he had.

Something warm was spilling out of his left side, although he didn't notice it.

That walk through the deserted countryside seemed to go on forever, but the sun still hadn't risen much when he stumbled over for the last time. He was thirsty, and he bit down on the dewy grass, then tried to get up, but couldn't. So he lay on his back, his arms stretched in the shape of a cross, at which point the liquid gushing out of his sides began spilling out faster.

The morning suddenly sprang to life. A suave lament hovered under the heavens, then shyly skimmed over the earth. Then it grew more intense. New calls added to it and reinforced it, propping it up, making it resonate in a deep, yet gentle manner. Without recognizing the sound as the song of bells coming from a nearby convent, calling the faithful to mass at dawn, Thélis welcomed their voice like a friend, like an ancient childhood lullaby.

Nor did he recognize the female choir that accompanied the chiming of cast iron and bronze, but he felt its sweetness wash over him.

He no longer lay in a field where a broken body had dragged him. Nor was it the sun that was kissing his face with its golden lips. The sky and the earth had fused together into a fluid expanse. He knew that his life had come to an end, and that the harmonized song of bells and human voices was greeting the liberation of his soul.

The captain stepped into that tender death while he was still alive.

*

When his remains were brought back to the squadron, none of the captain's comrades cried, but they all felt that the smile that had been too firmly drawn onto those lips, which had once been so cheerful, had carried away a very dear, pure and noble part of their youth with them.

CHAPTER XI

MARBOT REFUSED to go to the hospital before the funeral had taken place. Ravaged by a fever and with only a crude dressing covering his wounded shoulder, he kept watch over Thélis's body, refusing to allow anyone to approach the lifeless corpse. Only Herbillon was granted the privilege of spending a few moments next to the captain and to hear Marbot's lips tell the story of Thélis's last fight against five German planes.

When the cadet left the tent where the captain's body lay in repose, he heard the loud, animated voices of Reuillard and Doc. Maury had just been appointed squadron commander, and this didn't sit well with the old captain and the pilot-physician. The former believed the post should have gone to him considering he outranked Maury, whereas the latter thought it should have been bestowed on him due to his seniority. Seeing that anger allowed Jean to realize the squadron was already falling apart.

Its soul lay sleeping over there, where Marbot kept watch over it.

It received a new lease of life for a single morning, when the captain's funeral took place. Every man in the squadron—down to the lowliest mechanic—stood around the pit where the coffin was being lowered. Jean saw the most carefree and hardened of faces burst into tears, while his own remained welled up in his eyes, burning them.

When it was over, Herbillon headed out to the field with Maury, as they were scheduled to fly a mission. The same grief bowed their necks, since they had both, in their own unique way, loved Thélis. Claude murmured: "Let's try to be friends again, Jean."

Herbillon directed his gaze at him, which seemed devoid of all meaning.

"Let's not dwell on anything any more," he said. "Who knows how long we've got left?"

As though to silence everything within them that had rebelled against their friendship, Claude spoke of Thélis, and the tenderness they felt for him proved so great that they forgot their own troubles so they could focus their thoughts on their beloved captain. Yet to show how much suffering that death had caused him,

Claude felt compelled to say: "I received an incredibly anguished letter from Hélène; I didn't know I'd inspired such a love for Thélis in her."

Since Herbillon thought that keeping his mouth shut about it would betray the very memory of Thélis, he replied: "I was the one, who since my arrival here…"

He didn't dare finish his sentence. Claude felt as though the last dark curtain had finally lifted.

They didn't exchange a single word before climbing into their plane.

The cadet's fingers were riddled with icy needles as he tried to keep them moving in order to stave off the torturous cold. He knew he would have to endure this for some time as they were on their way back from a mission that had taken them very far past the German lines and, in order to reduce the risks, they'd flown at an altitude of 6,000 metres.

He'd been able to see some familiar sights again; the Aisne, Hill 108, and the plateau of Rosny, which was now occupied by the enemy. Yet his physical pain quickly replaced the melancholy that had moved in when confronted with the sight of the places where he'd been born into the life of the squadron, where Berthier, Deschamps and Thélis had come into his life, where he'd forged such a noble link with Maury, and finally where many of his illusions now lay buried.

A kind of yoke settled on his shoulders, seemingly stiffening his joints for good. The slightest movement required a disproportionate effort on his part. He felt as though his temples were caving under a weight that was becoming increasingly oppressive, and that was the source of the pain that kept hammering away at his head.

Maury's helmet and fur collar in front of him didn't seem to be moving at all. Sparing when it came to his own movements, feeling just as oppressed as Jean by the atmosphere, where the heart pumped away with difficulty, Maury's eyes were purely focused on ensuring the plane didn't lose any altitude.

At such heights, where the lines of the ground below barely appeared to move, it seemed that although its engine was working at fully capacity, the aircraft was hovering motionlessly in the air. The eyes always beheld the same, vast horizon, and the same immovable flat, green canvas, stitched with grey threads—roads—or blue ones—rivers.

From time to time, Herbillon would employ every iota of strength still left in him to stand up and observe the expanse of space before him. Habit governed his actions more than willpower. The torpor that permeated the whole of his being made him indifferent to the idea of danger. Claude felt a similar numbness.

Although their limbs were constricted by a morbid lethargy, their mental faculties were still intact. You might even say that the way their bodies abdicated their responsibilities endowed their thoughts with a crystal-clear lucidity, as well as freeing them from any negativity. Their minds could thus coolly and abstractedly analyse feelings that had usually caused them the greatest of suffering, right down to the very core of their beings.

Maury thus scientifically worked out the equation of his suffering.

Frame by frame, he visualized the first evening when Herbillon had come to him, how their friendship had ripened, how they had formed their crew, and finally how they'd forged that marvellous, mysterious bond that had linked their reflexes and intuitions.

Then there had been Herbillon's departure for Paris… his return… and the hell that followed. The hell where Maury had daily been forced to see his suspicions grow more accurate, deepen and be confirmed.

How could he have possibly convinced himself, purely to smother his suspicions, that the way Herbillon had behaved had been merely the product of a shy, nascent love? Truth be told, Claude had been very undemanding when it came to his need for happiness! The disappointment hadn't taken much time to unfold.

Now the conclusion had become all too obvious, and it was just as clear, icy and burdensome as that unbreathable air.

As though suddenly aware that Maury had crossed a forbidden line, Herbillon felt the irrepressible need to act. He stood up. He stretched his rebellious limbs. His gaze plunged to the ground below and, on seeing the river Vesle, he realized they would soon cross over into friendly skies. It was at this exact moment that the Drachen which had spotted their trajectory hurtled towards them at a sharp angle.

Jean wanted to shoot it down. With a sudden thrust, he altered the plane's delicate balance. Looking at Maury's eyes, which had reluctantly turned towards him, Jean had read the cool-headed assessment of their distressing situation, but he pointed to the captive balloon. Claude replied by way of an automatic, approving gesture.

The cadet already pictured the voluntary nosedive, when the engine's roar would suddenly break off, forcing the propeller to whirl like a vortex and hiss, the pleasant, dizzying anxiety that gripped the heart, the blazing bursts of gunfire against the Drachen's white target, and the parachute's slow, frail descent.

He crouched down inside the cockpit to create less wind resistance, when the mysterious flux that was proving both a curse and a blessing slid up against him from Claude's direction. He looked up and saw Maury's helmet tilting towards the ground. Heading in the same direction as his comrade's, Jean's younger eyes immediately noticed what had attracted the pilot's attention. Jean no longer felt cold.

Some brown spots seemed to be flying towards them from very far below. They looked like a swarm of midges, except for the fact that the sun often cast a sheen on them that Jean recognized as reflections bouncing off a metal surface. A German patrol was on the lookout, waiting for their return. Jean counted five planes and thought: "As many as the ones Thélis faced."

It looked as though they were climbing slowly, practically imperceptibly, but Herbillon, who'd learned to judge distances, knew that they would catch up to them before they crossed the Marne. They could only rely on a single hope: that the German fighters would be incapable of reaching their altitude.

Without either of them exchanging a signal, Maury hauled back on the stick to lift the nose in an attempt to gain even more altitude. All in vain: judging by the plane's sluggish reaction and the engine's breathlessness, they realized they'd reached an altitude they could not surpass. Nevertheless, the brown spots kept growing larger, and looking at their shorter wings and the stockier build of the new models, they gave up all hope of outrunning them. Those German fighters, flying more resiliently through that air than their heavier two-seater, still had an edge over them, even at those heights.

Despite the leaden weight that had settled on his limbs, Herbillon loaded his magazines and lowered the turret. The effort crippled his chest and left him feeling dizzy, but sitting upright, he thought: "Maury's got to pitch down. We'll be better able to fight that way."

As though answering his wish, an icy gust of wind burned his hands and the shock of the plane's abrupt descent cut off his breath. Claude was making the exact manoeuvre Jean had hoped for.

Finding itself back in denser air, the engine began to roar like thunder and the plane's tail, which now lay above the young man's head, looked like that of a mythical fish. Jean was being crushed against the side of the cockpit, tethered to his machine guns, keeping a lookout for the enemy.

Now the German patrol fell upon them at the speed of thought.

The purple bullets, the plane's jolting, the German fighters' vertiginous acrobatics, and that steel plate which Jean hugged to his chest as though it were a human being—all of these were the vital essence of the young man's life, for what seemed like seconds, or hours. Then the astonished euphoria of still being alive lifted his spirits. During that crazy dive which Maury had plunged the plane into, threatening to tear it apart in the process, they had crossed over the lines. Lady Luck had taken them under her wing. The Marne had turned visibly blue again. They would cross it in just a few seconds. They were saved.

Yet a cry burst out of Claude's mouth and, even though he didn't hear it, Jean felt as though his heart stopped still. There were three single-seater planes with black crosses on their wings heading from the direction of French skies. It was the second wave of attack, and the other fighters that had engaged them at first returned for another attack. The young man was overwhelmed by the enemy-studded sky. They didn't stand a chance while caught between those two agile, terrible waves. Maury tried his hardest to find a chink in that flying suit of armour which moved with lightning-speed strokes, yet each thrust their aeroplane made was met by an even more vigorous parry.

Herbillon passively waited for that terrible game to come to an end. How long would it last? Neither of them knew. They finally realized they were about to die.

At that moment, a kind of spasm took hold of Claude. He wanted to know. Although he'd come to an abstract conclusion, having heard the bell toll for him, his incredulity overruled his logic. At that defining moment, he still hoped that his friend hadn't betrayed him, and that his loyal wife would cry for him.

He couldn't leave that world without either being certain of his crewman's innocence, or hearing a fully fledged confession of betrayal. In a familiar gesture, he turned to look at Jean, who, sitting upright, had been waiting for Claude's gaze to meet his.

The bullets sketched a trail of fire above their heads. The drunken wind wounded them with its lashing gusts, and the engine's roar had synchronized with their blood, giving it a superhuman rhythm. Their nerves were more alive than ever, their senses sharper and their wits quicker. All because death had opened its mouth to swallow them up, and they could already smell its breath. They had now become a single mind in a single body.

Herbillon easily understood the reason behind the haunted look in Maury's eyes. The crew was headed to its demise, and Claude was demanding to know the truth. Jean knew he had no right to keep anything from the man who was going to sink into the vast expanse of the sky with him.

Yet Jean's fear of death was trumped by his fear of being hated by Claude. He wanted them to die in a brotherly manner, and for their crew to be finally reconciled. Under Claude's fixed state, Jean humbly joined his hands together.

Then he furiously grabbed hold of his machine-gun butts.

Maury automatically turned the plane on its side to prevent the fighter that was coming at him from below, which was wrapped a hail of sparks, from firing at him. The rabid pack of planes danced around him. His resistance was being guided solely by his instincts.

Maury was stunned by his dexterity at that moment, because Herbillon's gesture had made it clear that Jean simply wanted to die. Quick, quick, if only a bullet could put an end to the whirlwind of his thoughts!

Claude was possessed by such wrath that the thought that his disloyal friend would share his fate made him happy, and he even wanted to hasten their end.

When an enemy came at him again, Maury jerked the plane to the right, heading straight for the fighter, without even bothering to fire on him, certain he would smash it to pieces with the full force of his weight.

Yet a memory forced itself upon him. None of his other comrades had wanted him as their pilot, nobody except Herbillon. Was this how he was going to reward his trust?

A hard pull on the rudder allowed the plane to give way. The German plane passed so close by that Maury saw the enemy pilot let go of the controls and brace for impact. Taken aback by that desperate manoeuvre, and afraid that they might shoot at their comrade, the other fighters held their fire. The Marne—and, beyond it, salvation—was right there.

Yet Claude hesitated when it came to steering the plane towards it.

All of a sudden, he felt a sting on his side; and when he understood that a bullet had pierced him, he was stupefied and terrorized to feel the will to live rage within him.

Despite Jean's confession, and despite the loss of all hope, Claude didn't want to die. His teeth tore through his lips in order to overcome the weakness that was overwhelming him; his hand stiffened against the rudder which still miraculously governed the plane, and he dove towards safe ground. The kind of strength beasts experience when cornered and about to die led him to choose a suitable field and fulfil all the ritual manoeuvres that this entailed.

When the plane rolled along the thick grass, he turned towards Jean so he could vent his delirious, joyful cry. As the plane shook, a head bobbed about in the rear cockpit, one of its temples crowned with a sombre foam.

The sun spilled through the closed shutters, its dull light toned with amber highlights.

It didn't hurt Claude's eyes when they opened after he'd lain unconscious for sixteen days. He noticed a figure sitting down next to his bed, its head hung low. The robe it was wearing cast a shadow against the white walls. The way its shoulders curved and the simplicity of its hairdo allowed Claude to recognize it as Hélène.

Yet her beatitude was so frail and calm that Claude didn't dare disturb it by moving and he shut his eyes. A fever grazed his skin, light as a caress. Claude wanted nothing more than to prolong that moment, when the happiness of his reconquered life flowed according to a divine rhythm.

However, despite himself, Claude looked at Hélène, who hadn't stirred at all. He couldn't see any of her face except for her smooth forehead and the distinct curve of her hair. How close they were, and yet how far. How vague and insignificant she seemed to him! Looking at her, Claude felt the intense desire for his resurrection to be greeted by a different face.

The image of a tender, male face flashed confusedly across the limbo of his mind. Herbillon! But why was there a red aureola around his temple?

His bated breath grew more urgent! He began to relive the entire experience: the dogfight, the terror of death, the euphoria of salvation, the desire to share it all with his comrade. Then the vision of that vacated body which had torn him apart.

Who was Hélène thinking about as she sat there completely still? Jean, of course. She was right! Just moments after they'd succumbed to the beating of those funereal wings, all that suspicion and suffering had seemed so pitiful! How could he have entrusted his will to live to those petty sentiments?

Now that he'd left the kingdom of shadows, he knew…

Herbillon! His young face, his young body! How he'd sadly joined his hands together up there in that deadly sky!

Claude's chest was empty except for a heartbroken pity.

When Hélène finally raised her face, an etching of sorrow, she found a set of bright eyes staring at her. She started to move towards him, but he gestured to her with his eyelids, signalling that she should stop.

"Where did they bury him?" he asked, in a murmur so low she had to bend over to hear him.

As though following her own train of thought, she answered: "Next to the captain."

"That's good."

Exhausted, Claude fell silent again. A fly fluttered in the air like a wild bullet. His eyes followed it as it rushed around, then his gaze fell on Hélène once again. The tears she was holding back were shining through her eyelashes.

"Go ahead, cry, cry," he told her, "I so wish that I could."

She knew that he knew, and shamefully took his hand in hers. He clenched her cool hand. Then her head dropped onto the sheets and her shoulders heaved with sobs.

The line formed by her neck was so full and solid, and her despair so vibrant with youth, that a pensive smile formed on Claude's lips. Hélène would forget all about Officer Cadet Jean Herbillon long before he did.

LA VALLÉE-AUX-LOUPS

4 SEPTEMBER 1923

Pushkin Press

Pushkin Press was founded in 1997, and publishes novels, essays, memoirs, children's books—everything from timeless classics to the urgent and contemporary.

This book is part of the Pushkin Collection of paperbacks, designed to be as satisfying as possible to hold and to enjoy. It is typeset in Monotype Baskerville, based on the transitional English serif typeface designed in the mid-eighteenth century by John Baskerville. It was litho-printed on Munken Premium White Paper and notch-bound by the independently owned printer TJ International in Padstow, Cornwall. The cover, with French flaps, was printed on Colorplan Pristine White paper. The paper and cover board are both acid-free and Forest Stewardship Council (FSC) certified.

Pushkin Press publishes the best writing from around the world—great stories, beautifully produced, to be read and read again.

STEFAN ZWEIG · EDGAR ALLAN POE · ISAAC BABEL
TOMÁS GONZÁLEZ · ULRICH PLENZDORF · TEFFI
VELIBOR ČOLIĆ · LOUISE DE VILMORIN · MARCEL AYMÉ
ALEXANDER PUSHKIN · MAXIM BILLER · JULIEN GRACQ
BROTHERS GRIMM · HUGO VON HOFMANNSTHAL
GEORGE SAND · PHILIPPE BEAUSSANT · IVÁN REPILA
E.T.A. HOFFMANN · ALEXANDER LERNET-HOLENIA
YASUSHI INOUE · HENRY JAMES · FRIEDRICH TORBERG
ARTHUR SCHNITZLER · ANTOINE DE SAINT-EXUPÉRY
MACHI TAWARA · GAITO GAZDANOV · HERMANN HESSE
LOUIS COUPERUS · JAN JACOB SLAUERHOFF
PAUL MORAND · MARK TWAIN · PAUL FOURNEL
ANTAL SZERB · JONA OBERSKI · MEDARDO FRAILE
HÉCTOR ABAD · PETER HANDKE · ERNST WEISS
PENELOPE DELTA · RAYMOND RADIGUET · PETR KRÁL
ITALO SVEVO · RÉGIS DEBRAY · BRUNO SCHULZ